"I feel the snow." Bleu's joy was palpable, and he stuck out his tongue to catch snowflakes.

Ryan laughed, delighted. "What does it feel like, babe?"

"Tiny kisses."

"Mmm. Cold kisses." He chuckled some more, opening the car door for Bleu.

"Uh-huh. But they're sweet enough, right?"

"Right." He wanted to kiss that mouth, but he didn't dare. Bleu wasn't with him on that yet.

Welcome to
Dreamspun Desires

Dear Reader,

Love is the dream. It dazzles us, makes us stronger, and brings us to our knees. Dreamspun Desires tell stories of love featuring your favorite heartwarming heroes, captivating plots, and exotic locations. Stories that make your breath catch and your imagination soar.

In the pages of these wonderful love stories, readers can escape to a world where love conquers all, the tenderness of a first kiss sweeps you away, and your heart pounds at the sight of the one you love.

When you put it all together, you find romance in its truest form.

Love always finds a way.

Elizabeth North

Executive Director
Dreamspinner Press

BA Tortuga

WHISKEY TO WINE

PUBLISHED BY

Published by
DREAMSPINNER PRESS

5032 Capital Circle SW, Suite 2, PMB# 279,
Tallahassee, FL 32305-7886 USA
www.dreamspinnerpress.com

This is a work of fiction. Names, characters, places, and incidents either are the product of author imagination or are used fictitiously, and any resemblance to actual persons, living or dead, business establishments, events, or locales is entirely coincidental.

Paperback ISBN: 978-1-64108-106-1
Digital ISBN: 978-1-64080-771-6
Library of Congress Control Number: 2018940823
Paperback published March 2019
v. 1.0

Printed in the United States of America
∞
This paper meets the requirements of
ANSI/NISO Z39.48-1992 (Permanence of Paper).

BA TORTUGA, Texan to the bone and an unrepentant Daddy's Girl, spends her days with her basset hounds, getting tattooed, texting her sisters, and eating Mexican food. When she's not doing that, she's writing. She spends her days off watching rodeo, knitting, and surfing Pinterest in the name of research. BA's personal saviors include her wife, Julia Talbot, her best friend, Sean Michael, and coffee. Lots of coffee. Really good coffee.

Having written everything from fist-fighting rednecks to hard-core cowboys to werewolves, BA does her damnedest to tell the stories of her heart, which was raised in Northeast Texas, but has heard the call of the high desert and lives in the Sandias. With books ranging from hard-hitting GLBT romance, to fiery ménages, to the most traditional of love stories, BA refuses to be pigeonholed by anyone but the voices in her head.

Website: www.batortuga.com
Blog: batortuga.blogspot.com
Facebook: www.facebook.com/batortuga
Twitter: @batortuga

By BA Tortuga

DREAMSPUN DESIRES
#6 – Trial by Fire
#30 – Two Cowboys and a Baby
#65 – Two of a Kind

LEANING N
#16 – Commitment Ranch
#42 – Finding Mr. Wright
#78 – Whiskey to Wine

TURQUOISE, NEW MEXICO
#53 – Cowboy in the Crosshairs

Published by **DREAMSPINNER PRESS**
www.dreamspinnerpress.com

To my girl.

Prologue

STONEY didn't know about this whole "bring a blind man to the stables" thing, but Ford said this guy needed to see a horse, and he'd be damned if he was going to let someone else be in charge of that.

If someone was fixin' to get into big trouble, it might as well be him.

He stroked Copper's face, the big old gelding the most easygoing of them all. "You'd best be nice, old man. This guy's like some Santa Fe artist that makes my Ford about stupid with joy."

Copper bobbed his head as if nodding, blowing those big lips at him. Yeah, Copper knew his job.

He heard the scrape of Ford's boots on the gravel outside the barn. "Here we go, bud."

A tall, buff blond with dark glasses and a great smile appeared in the doorway, holding on to a lovely Native American guy. Pretty.

"Hey, y'all. I'm Stoney River, Ford's husband."

"Pleased. This is Bleu Bridey. I'm Dan Klah." The bolo tie of silver and enormous turquoise spoke of relative wealth, and the guy had Navajo written all over him, from the raven wing hair to the cheekbones you could ski off.

"Pleased, y'all. So, you want to learn about horses."

"I need to see one. Touch one. I can hear it breathing," Bleu said.

"Him."

"What?"

Stoney grinned. "Copper's a him. He's a nine-year-old gelding. He loves to meet people."

"Oh." Bleu's cheeks went pink. "Right."

"Here, take my hand and I'll ease you in." He held Copper by the halter firmly while reaching out for Bleu.

Dan put Bleu's hand in his, so Stoney waited for the feller to step close.

"This is a little unnerving," Bleu admitted.

"Sure it is, because he's a big old thing, but he's gentle. He's a good boy." And the guy needed to chill, because Copper knew he was okay.

"Okay." Bleu put his hand where Stoney directed it, right on Copper's nose. "So soft!"

"I'm going to lead your hand at first, just so you don't get his eyes."

"Thanks. I don't want to hurt him."

His level of respect jumped up. "I appreciate that."

"He sounds impatient. That's his hooves on the floor, right?"

Stoney laughed. "He's just shifting his weight. If he was impatient, he'd be swishing his tail or nibbling you."

He showed Bleu the heavy cheeks, the way that Copper's head flattened out over his forehead, the little swirl of hair at Copper's forelock.

Copper took it all for long moments before he started snuffling at Bleu's shirt pockets.

"Would you like to give him a carrot?"

"Can I?"

"Sure, I need you to…. Uh…." Stoney stretched out his fingers, trying to explain. "Make your hand flat and keep it that way."

"Like this?" Bleu held up a hand, palm up, fingers extended.

"Just that way. Now, make sure you keep your fingers flat." He dropped a cut carrot on Bleu's palm.

Copper nibbled it up, velvety soft lips teasing Bleu's skin.

Bleu laughed out loud. "Feel that! He's very sweet."

"It's like velvet, isn't it? So soft. His lips come up to his nostrils."

"He's giving me goose bumps." Bleu drew away. "Can I lean on him?"

"You can." This was way better than Stoney had worried it would be. Seeing Copper through a blind guy's touch was really neat.

Bleu rested against Copper's neck, expression pure wonder. "Oh God. Dan. Dan, I can hear his heart."

"He's gorgeous, Bleu. Deep in the chest, long in the legs. He's this rich, glorious color with a white blaze down his nose." The Dan guy sounded like he knew his way around a horse.

Copper lipped at Bleu's shoulder curiously, but stayed calm like the practiced trail horse he was.

"His mane is like his tail, coarser, and his ears are so soft."

Stoney just stood and watched, guiding Bleu every so often to touch somewhere else. This was the best part of his job; he got a huge kick introducing people to ranch life.

Periodically he'd see Ford watching him with this goofy-assed look on his face.

Stoney did adore that. God, he loved his life.

"Thank you for this. Seriously. I needed to see this."

"Not a problem. If you want to try riding, Copper is your guy. I can take you out anytime while you're here, as long as the weather is good."

"Really?"

"Absolutely. I live for this shit."

The Dan guy laughed. "You do, huh?"

"Yep. That and my husband and son." Stoney winked over but realized Bleu would miss that.

"I can't think of anything better. Oh, Dan, I do love it here."

"Hey, I thought you would. I chose well." Dan winked back at Stoney. "Inspiration."

"I have to appreciate anyone who's inspired by the Leanin' N."

"Well, I am. I would love to go riding tomorrow," Bleu said.

"Sure. How long are y'all staying?"

"A week or so." Dan grinned. "We'll see."

"That's a good amount of time."

"Yeah. I wanted immersion." Bleu shrugged. "And the food is amazing."

"I love the meatloaf best, but pizza is a huge favorite."

"I loved that brown sugar pie thing," Bleu murmured.

Stoney grinned and nodded. "You've had the coffee?"

Bleu leaned against him, easy as pie, unselfconscious as anything. “Oh my God, better than sex.”

“You know it.”

Both Dan and Ford went “Hey” at the same time.

Stoney snapped his teeth at Ford, teasing. “We should go have some. Coffee, I mean.”

Bleu’s laughter was loud enough that Copper tossed his head. “Coffee sounds great.”

“Okay. Dan, can you help guide Bleu out so I can give Copper here some oats?”

At the word oats, Copper shifted his weight hard, and Bleu staggered, laughing again when Dan caught him.

Stoney did appreciate a guest with a sense of humor. Around the ranch, a guy needed one or he’d always be mad.

“Coffee sounds good,” Ford said, leading the others off.

“Come on, buddy, let’s get you some oats.” Stoney got to work, whistling as he did.

He loved the ranch almost as much as he did Ford and Quartz. Almost. They were all part of it.

It was in his blood, these days.

He finished up before hurrying back to the house.

Stoney didn’t want to miss that coffee.

Chapter One

"ARE we there yet?"

"What? Are you five, man?" Dan's voice was warm, amused. "The weather is a little challenging, you know?"

"Well, I can see the snow building up everywhere…." The sarcasm was tempered by his good mood. Bleu chuckled. Snow was good, though. The big reveal of his sculpture for the Leaning N coincided with the opening of ski season and the big gay ski gala.

He'd been tickled as all get-out when Ford Nixel had asked him for a statue for Stoney and the Leaning N. Stoney had taught him about horses, about cowboys, about barns and hay and saddles.

He felt like family at the Leaning N, as if he would always have a place there.

"You're just wanting Geoff's pizza."

"You know it. You think he's too busy getting ready for the party to make it?" He could live a lifetime on that shit. Sausage flatbread….

"I bet he has one vegan and two meat lover's waiting for us."

"Thanks for bringing me and Floyd up, Dan. I know you didn't have to." It was funny, the things that caused a relationship to break apart—money, infidelity, an allergy to your Seeing Eye dog.

Dan was still one of his best friends, though, and he adored the ranch too.

"Hey, I wasn't gonna miss that coffee."

"The cinnamon latte…." He leaned against Dan, the solid body so strong beside him.

"Yeah. With a tiny bit of Fireball…." Dan didn't drink hardly at all, but he did like a bit of hot stuff.

"Hell yeah. You know how I feel about the burn." Bleu got off on it.

"I know. Such an experience whore." Dan nuzzled his hair briefly. "I love the N, as you are well aware. Like I was going to say no."

"I know. Still, I appreciate it. Stoney's going to shit when he sees what Ford's done."

"I hope not. That sounds like hell."

"Right." God, Dan was a dear man, but… sometimes Bleu just wanted to be crass and not perfectly reasonable. He hated having to censor his humor, which was… well, his theory was people with physical limitations could be a little off-color.

Off-color. He snorted, the pun amusing the fuck out of him.

"You coming down with something?" Dan asked.

"Nope. I was amusing myself, since I don't seem to amuse you." He kept it light, but God knew it was the truth.

"Stop it. You know I adore you."

"I do." He patted Dan's leg. "I wouldn't know what to do without you as my friend."

"You'd have to find a driver, of course, and someone to call when you can't identify a sound in your house."

"Right?" He would have to do all that again once Dan found another lover, but for now, they had a system.

"The landscape is changing. I'm glad we stopped and had chains put on."

"Yeah. I guess it gets rough up here." Bleu wanted to feel the difference in the snow, one from the other.

"Deep, you know?"

"Yeah. Like the ski mountain." He clapped his hands. "Which is why we're here, right?"

"Yeah. You're really considering skiing?"

"I am. How impossible can it be?"

"You can't see, you know, Bleu."

"Oh my God!" he proclaimed. "I can't?"

"Oh, stop, you could kill yourself running into a tree."

"I could die falling out of the bed, from a heart attack, a giant alligator attack."

Dan snorted. "You could, but you have a dog for the first, and where are you going to find a gator?"

"I bet you can buy them on Amazon."

Dan hooted. "They have them at the zoo in 'Burque."

"They have them at that weird snake museum on the other side of Austin."

"Right." Dan laughed harder. "No killing yourself, regardless."

Bleu laughed softly. "You worry too much, honey."

"I always do." They turned off, the direction change and road texture obvious.

"We're heading up, right?"

"To the ranch, yeah." Dan hummed with the radio, and Bleu was a little glad it was past Christmas music. Dan was an addict.

Ford had asked him for a sculpture of him and Stoney together, the ranch and horses added in. He'd thought about it for a few months, and then he did an amalgam of the guys' hands, the ranch, and a horse.

It had been a task, keeping it secret from Stoney. There had been a lot of spontaneous "looking" with his fingers and making Stoney believe he was just… kinda forgetful.

Thank goodness Ford always had business to do in Santa Fe and could bring Stoney to him. Bleu loved going, doing, but life was easier in his little adobe house and studio, where he might be bored, but he rarely face-planted. Floyd helped with that out and about, but home was so many paces by so many, and he banged his shins less.

He grinned. Good thing he couldn't see the bruises to mind.

"What's funny?" Dan asked.

"I was just thinking how many times I had to feel up Stoney."

"He's very taken, you know."

"I totally know. Completely." Stoney was the most taken. The takenest. He and Ford… well, you could feel the energy between them on the air. He didn't need to see it.

It reminded him a lot of him and…. No. No thinking about that. No borrowing trouble.

He didn't need to open up even more old wounds.

"Now you're frowning." Dan touched his leg again, the contact comforting. "You okay?"

His face always gave him away. Bleu had no way to school it.

"Just fine. Ready to get out of the car."

"Well, we just crested that long rise, and I can see the ranch." Dan was always willing to be sympathetic. He was a good man.

"Is it beautiful? Is it…?" He had to imagine how it was, because he had no true concept of colors, of shadow. Those would have to be appreciated by everyone else.

"It's amazing. The sky goes on forever, and the mountains rise up all around like sentries. It's cloudy, so there are all these moving shapes that change as we drive."

"Oh…." God, sometimes it hurt, how much he wanted to see like everyone else.

"It's kinda like one of your sculptures." They coasted to a stop, and he could hear hustle and bustle as soon as they opened the doors.

He went to get Floyd and harnessed his good friend up. They would navigate the landscape here together. He was amazed Dan wasn't sneezing.

Good thing they had a two-bedroom cabin this visit.

"Bleu! There you are. Thank God you had chains." Ford came out to meet them.

"Dan's always prepared. Always." He reached out, and Ford gave him the hug he wanted. "I love being here. It feels like home."

"Thank you. You're part of the family, man." Ford was a great hugger. "Did you have a good Christmas?"

"I did. It was cozy and quiet. Me and my folks." They'd had posole and tamales and biscochitos, just like always. It had been grand.

"We had a ton of guests." Ford let him go, presumably to hug Dan. "Geoff was in heaven. He mastered high altitude soufflé."

"Oh wow." He wasn't sure what that was, but if it had to be mastered, it had to be hard.

Dan laughed. "Oh man, I love a chocolate soufflé."

They started moving, and Floyd kept him in pace and on track. The snow underfoot crunched instead of swooshing, so it had to have been really wet and heavy.

When they got settled, he'd ask if Quartz could come play. He did love snow. So did Floyd. Dan, not so much.

"Hey!" A wave of warmth hit them, and Floyd guided him up the kitchen steps. He was enveloped in a hug that smelled like flour, cinnamon, and cloves. Geoff.

"Geoff! My friend!" He buried his nose in Geoff's neck, inhaling deep. He loved when people let him touch, let him in to see.

"How are you? Hey, Dan." Geoff never let go, though, just gave him the best hug ever.

"Hey there. Smells like heaven in here, sir."

"Thanks! I'm trying a new cinnamon roll recipe."

"Ooh. Big gooey ones?"

"God yes. I like the icing I normally use, but the dough gets… weird up this high."

He let Geoff go. "I needed that. Thank you."

"No problem." Geoff guided him to a chair. "Floyd, my boy, I have a treat for you."

He felt Floyd's tail banging on his leg. Someone liked those words. "Sit, boy. You can have a treat." Floyd was working, so permission was important. Geoff was good about it.

Floyd sat with a thump, and Bleu suddenly smelled peanut butter.

Then he heard Floyd licking and licking. Ah, a Kong.

"You spoil him." He had to laugh; here, he was family.

"I know, but he's a good boy. Did I ever tell you about the basset who came for a wedding?"

"Bassets… long ears?"

"Lots of drool. Short legs." Geoff handed him a cup of coffee, lifting his hand to feel it.

"Oh, thank you. No, tell me everything."

"Oh my God. He was the cutest old thing…." Geoff told him about this amazing redneck wedding and how many of the guests hooked up.

He had coffee, a cinnamony sweet, good friends, music. It was magic.

The crunch of gravel outside told him someone new had arrived. Ford made a *huh* kind of noise. "Is someone else scheduled to come in?"

"We have people straggling in for Ski Week all week long, Ford."

"But I thought I had set it up so only Bleu arrived this afternoon." The air moved when Ford rose. "Be right back."

"He worries." Stoney sat close. "Have you been busy?"

"I have. Good busy, though. I love my job." Sculpting made him happy, balls to bones.

"I bet. It's so tactile." Stoney had opened up a lot for him once they started riding horses together.

"I think you would like it, man. I think you'd enjoy it."

"Yeah? I've got a lot to do, honey." Stoney was so… Texan.

"You don't have a couple hours to play? You and Ford could do it together."

"We'll try it, then. I mean, not until after ski weekend."

"Sure. You're going to be busy."

"You'll be leaving with me on Sunday, Bleu, don't forget." Right. Dan had to be… somewhere.

"Maybe another time, then."

"Totally." Stoney touched the back of his hand.

The door opened, a cold wave of air coming in. "Oh God, what smells so good in here?"

Bleu tilted his head. He knew that voice. He knew it, bone-deep.

Ryan.

Ryan "I Fucked Up Your Life And Left You Heartbroken" Shields.

Goddamn.

Chapter Two

RYAN stepped into the kitchen of the Leaning N, and the smell of cinnamon rolls hit him in the face. "Oh God, what smells so good in here? Hey, Geoff. Stoney…."

There was a long, long moment of silence. "Hey, Bleu."

Bleu Bridey. Right there in the flesh. Long, dark blond hair, broad shoulders, cheekbones sharp enough to cut diamonds. Damn.

He'd never thought he would see that man again.

"Hey. This is Dan, and the dog is Floyd."

"Hi, uh, Dan." He shook the stocky Native American guy's hand.

"Pleased to meet you."

Bleu sat there, still and quiet, head tilted. Bleu had always been able to pull inside himself and make Ryan feel… alone.

"How's everyone?" he asked, his country polite upbringing kicking in.

"Good. Good. Coffee?" Stoney grinned at him, the man offering him a cup before he answered. Texans and their coffee.

"God, please. It was a drive." He'd come down from Steamboat after doing a bit of an exhibition.

"Yeah, the roads are something else. You staying for the week, huh?"

"I am." He was staring at Bleu. He knew he was staring, but he couldn't help it. God, the man was still… ethereal and beautiful, and those hands had…. Damn.

Those sculptor's hands had given him hours of pleasure.

"So is Phil not coming up?" Ford asked him.

"Huh? Oh, uh, he'll be up Wednesday. Flying into Aspen." Phil was still a business contact, but no longer a personal one.

"Good deal. We're planning one hell of a party. I can't wait." Ford was looking from him to Bleu, gaze sharp.

"Cool. Geoff, that smells good."

"Cinnamon rolls. You want one?"

"I do." He didn't want to sit there with ever-so-silent Bleu, though. "You mind if I take it to the great room? I need to plug in my phone."

"Of course not."

"Dan, we should go to our cabin, huh?" Bleu stood, reaching for the German shepherd at his side. "Let Stoney and Ford get back to work."

"Oh. Sure." Dan sure didn't have a poker face. "See you guys later."

"I'll take y'all down to your cabin. Make sure all is well." Stoney stood and offered him a grin. "I'll leave you with Ford and Geoff."

"Sure. Thanks." He breathed deep, inhaling the coffee.

As soon as the door closed, Ford said, "Is there a story there?"

"Huh?" Ryan widened his eyes, trying for innocent.

"Oh, you can't fool us! We're bored and dying for gossip." Geoff placed a plate of sticky gooey goodness in front of him.

Ryan contemplated running, but he really needed to tell someone. "Bleu and I were a thing. Like a big-time thing."

"No shit?" Ford plopped down. "Geoff, get the Baileys."

"On it, boss."

Ryan chuckled. "Oh, good idea."

"Man, I'm a fan of booze for stories."

"I bet you are. Freaks." He winked at Geoff, who didn't partake of the alcohol but sat with a cup of rooibos tea.

"Tell," Geoff said.

"We met in college, believe it or not. Freshman year. Lived together in the dorms, then in an apartment." They'd been wild for each other, for fun and parties and sex in every way possible. They'd been like whiskey, burning all the way down.

Geoff propped his elbows on the table. "What happened?"

"We were gasoline and matches, I guess. We graduated and started having to look for jobs." He hadn't been ready for it, the complications of living with a blind man. At college they'd been surrounded with friends, with a companion assistant for Bleu.

In the real life, Bleu'd been scared, Ryan had been frustrated, and they'd ended up tearing each other to shreds.

"So it ended badly," Geoff said.

"Hoo yeah."

"He seems like a decent guy, and I know you are…." Ford sounded so confused.

"We were young and kinda idiots. You don't have to take sides." Ryan snorted. "You might have to run interference."

"I can do that. Bleu spends most of his time here trying to learn something new. He's actually a shockingly good rider."

"That doesn't surprise me." He sort of kept tabs, a little. He knew Bleu had gotten engaged to a high-dollar type. Hell, maybe they were married already. "He was always pretty gifted physically."

When Geoff and Ford both stared at him wordlessly, he flushed, his cheeks hot as fire. "Stop it."

"I didn't say a word," Ford said, but it was Geoff who had the wildly gyrating eyebrows.

"Is it true? Are his other senses more tuned in?"

"Uh. Yes." And he could totally say that not in relation to sex. In relation to sex? Jesus. Bleu was the best he'd ever, ever had.

Still.

"That's so neat." Geoff got the conversation back on the rails. "I'll have to be careful not to mutter around him."

"Yeah, although he used to be good about pretending not to overhear things." Bleu had really had him fooled. He'd been trying to figure out how to move out without hurting Bleu's feelings, how to break it off without leaving

Bleu in the lurch, and he'd come home to an empty house, a note outlining all the things Bleu had overheard.

God, he'd felt like shit, and he'd missed the man. As he'd gotten older, though, he'd gotten mad. Bleu had known and hadn't been invested enough to fight for them.

Then he'd… well, he'd found the life he'd wanted. X Games, ski instructor, sponsorships, and then he started designing snowboards, skis. He didn't have the time to worry about a man who needed as much assistance as Bleu did, no matter how amazing the sex had been.

Ryan refused to feel guilty. Guilt and regret were overrated.

Bleu was fine—an artist, married to a classy gallery owner, wealthy and respected. Bleu hadn't needed him.

All these years later, Ryan wasn't sure he'd ever stopped needing Bleu.

Shit.

"Hey, Ryan? It's okay, huh? Seriously. Old flames are just that. Old." Geoff squeezed his wrist.

"Right. I just need to get through ski weekend, anyway, huh? Lots of stress." This was a busy time of year for him.

"Yes, Mr. Celebrity. We're so glad you're here."

"I am too." He would be, anyway.

"Good. I gave you a cabin where you could ski out. It's private, and there's plenty of room for Phil when he gets here."

"Oh, he didn't mention?" Shit. Phil was supposed to say they needed separate lodging.

"Mention?" Ford looked to Geoff, then grabbed his phone. "Mention what?"

"We're not… not for almost six months." Shit.

"Oh, Jesus. I—let me grab Stoney and see what I need to do."

"Thanks." He gave Ford an apologetic look. The Leaning N wasn't exactly a huge resort kind of thing.

"I… we may have to put him in a hotel in Aspen. Maybe in a room here in the main house…."

"No. No, I know how busy you are. Can you get us an extra bed? Or a fold-out? I can sleep anywhere." He would share with Phil, just not sleep with him. They weren't together that way.

"There's two beds in your cabin—that's not an issue."

"Then we can totally share. Don't worry about it." He shared hotels on the road all the time. What could it hurt?

"Are you sure? Because Stoney's sending me to our office manager, Miranda, in a panic."

"No, I'm sure. Don't rearrange everyone for this." He and Phil weren't enemies; they just weren't… compatible.

They were business associates, and friendly, but well…. Could a man be friends with an ex?

He wasn't sure. Hell, he wasn't sure he and Phil had ever been friends.

When Ford gave him a panicky look, he just smiled. "Hey. At least I'm not having to room with Bleu."

"Yeah, Bleu's cabin is full."

"Well, there you go." Yeah, he'd assumed so. Why wouldn't Bleu be taken? The man was talented and good in bed. So what if he was a fuck?

Ryan ate his cinnamon roll because now he needed to reward himself.

"So, tell me you're looking forward to this week, at least?"

"Huh? Oh, totally. I make a third of my sales all year in this week."

"No shit?" Ford actually looked shocked. "I mean, it's a fabulous week for us, but…."

"Yep. I mean, snowboards and equipment are investments. I sell a lot to the tour, but to the general public? Christmas and ski week."

"That's great. We've got the cross-country skis for guests, but I keep trying to convince Stoney to try downhill. So far, no go."

"He might like snowboarding. The center of balance is better." He loved his sport.

"But I want to teach him."

Ah. Ryan got that. "I can teach you in secret, maybe after ski week."

"Oh." Ford lit up. "I would love that."

"Rock on." Ford was damn good to him. This would be something he could do that was special.

"We'll make a plan." Ford winked.

Geoff rolled his eyes. "Just don't be so sneaky that Stoney gets all freaked-out. You know how he can be. He has anxiety issues."

Ford chuckled. "I overthink; he overworries."

"Right." Geoff nodded firmly.

"I'll be sure to make it look unsuspicious." He winked over. "You can help me with marketing, O Marketing Wonder."

"I can so do that." Ford grinned. "Or, you know, look at legal things."

"Absolutely. Trademarks. Copyrights. Fun stuff."

"See?" Ford waggled his eyebrows. "I got all these skills."

"Totally. All that college edu-ma-cation."

"Right, what did you major in? Snow?"

Ryan snorted. "I majored in party. Seriously, though, I majored in recreation and outdoor education."

"I can see it, you partying. You have the best laugh."

God, Geoff was a sweetheart.

"Thanks, man." He smiled at Geoff, because the guy was all about joy.

"Anytime. Seriously. Are you coming up for supper, or do you have plans in town?"

"I would like to, but I don't want to make anyone uncomfortable." Maybe he would go to Aspen.

"Dan and Bleu don't eat in the dining room. We'll take them their plates."

"Oh. I can see that." Bleu would find a noisy dining room full of ski people chaotic. Dan, huh. Same guy was in the society pages, so they must have gotten married.

"Yeah, right? He'll eat in here with me sometimes, but only if it's just family."

"Right. Well, then count on me for supper." He was both disappointed and relieved.

"Good deal. Any requests?"

"Oh, you know I love anything you put out, Geoff." Pizza. Chicken wings. Crispy tofu with coconut rice.

"I do. I'm thinking stew with cornbread."

"Oh, I would love that."

"Then that's what it'll be." Geoff kissed his cheek. "Another cinnamon roll?"

"Oh God. I shouldn't." It wasn't like he was on tour anymore, and he would get time on the slopes this week, so…. "Yes."

"Ford?"

"God, Stoney's going to tease me mercilessly about my potbelly."

"Do eeeet," Ryan joshed.

"I'll do an extra hour on the treadmill in the morning…." Ford nodded. "Bring it on."

They all laughed, and Geoff moved to dish up more ooey-gooey cinnamon rolls.

God, this was why this place was famous—the generosity of the people.

The rest would work itself out.

Chapter Three

"WHO was that?" Dan asked, pouncing as soon as Bleu walked out of the master bedroom.

"Who was who?"

"Don't. You have no poker face. You looked… wounded."

He didn't even understand what poker face meant, not really. "I'm fine. We were in college together, that's all."

"And what did you do together while in college?" Dan moved closer, the air smelling like Acqua di Gió.

Made love for hours. "We were on Team Party. There was lots of beer involved."

"And nookie?" The incongruity of Dan saying "nookie" slayed him.

"Yeah. There was some of that too."

But Ryan had lost his mind, the summer after graduation, calling his folks and his sister constantly, stressing out about the "complications" of living with a blind man without the benefit of a full-time assistant, worrying about how he was supposed to take care of Bleu.

Take care of him. Like he was helpless or stupid or incapable of functioning. He'd been blind his whole life. He could manage just fine. If the man had just talked to him about it, instead of everyone else, they might have been able to work it out, but Ryan had withdrawn more and more, and Bleu hadn't been able to figure out what to do.

So he'd left.

He'd hired a car to take him to Santa Fe, contacted the Commission for the Blind, and he hit the ground running.

Well, hit the ground limping, but he'd managed.

Ryan had gone on to be hugely successful in his chosen sport, so Bleu guessed maybe it had worked out best for both of them.

Bleu didn't need a lover who thought he was a burden, no matter how hot they'd burned. Or not hot. God knew he and Dan had been placid, but Dan was also worried about him eating in public or trying to do anything physical.

Dan was best as a good friend and a hell of a gallery owner.

"Huh, you never looked like that about me, Bleu."

"You're making a lot of assumptions."

"I guess I am. Is it going to make you too weird? Being here at the same time as him?"

"It's not like I ever have to see him, honey." He amused the fuck out of himself.

"Oh, right." Dan always sounded so self-conscious when he made blind jokes.

"I… I'm going to go read, I guess." He wanted to go out, talk to people, explore, but… yeah. Later. Maybe when Dan left to do business. He didn't want to stress out his ex. Either one.

"Do you want me to order our food, then?"

"Why don't you go to the dining room without me?" He could call Stoney and go have supper with him and Quartz and Geoff while Ford was playing host.

"You don't mind?" Oh, Dan was eager, probably wanting to suss out Ryan.

"Not at all. I'm going to rest. Have fun, Dan."

"Thanks, honey." Dan bent to kiss his cheek before hustling off.

He waited for the door to close before dialing Stoney's number. While it rang, he fed Floyd, the big pup's tail banging against the counter in the little kitchenette.

"Hey, Bleu. Are you ready to order supper?"

"Uh… I was wondering if, well, can I share a meal with y'all? I mean, if you have an extra seat…." God, this was embarrassing, but he wanted to be able to relax and not be all alone.

"Oh! In the family dining room? You know it. Dan is…."

"He's eating in the main room. I just… I wanted to impose, which sucks for y'all, but obviously not enough I didn't do it."

"No imposition at all, honey. You need someone to come get you? Doogie or Tanner will, either one. Quartz is finishing up some homework."

"I can do it, I think."

"Okay, but if I don't see you in ten minutes, I'm coming to get you. Fair?"

"Fair." He loved that about Stoney, that he just believed Bleu and Floyd were a fine team.

"Remember, you're in the first cabin. The main house is ahead and—"

"To the left. I remember."

"Cool. Holler if you need us." Stoney hung up, and Bleu knew he needed to make sure Floyd did his thing too.

He got his coat on, his boots, and once Floyd was back in from his potty break, harnessed up his best friend. "Okay, let's go."

Floyd was immediately back in work mode. He responded to Bleu pointing him toward the main house, then steadily led Bleu around impediments.

He could feel the snowflakes kissing his cheeks, and it made him laugh, the tiny little touches. So cold, and yet so easy to melt with the heat from his skin. Floyd shook his head, his ears flapping.

"What are you doing out by yourself?"

The words surprised him, and he tilted his head. "I'm sorry?"

"You need some help? I thought you had a man to help out."

Oh, Ryan.

"I'm good." The house was forward and to the left.

"You sure?"

"Floyd is better at this than Ben ever was." Ben had been his college assistant.

"Okay. I just—"

"I'm good. Seriously." And even if he wasn't, he wouldn't admit it.

"The dining room is the other way."

"I've got a meeting with the owners." He kept moving.

"Oh." Did Ryan sound disappointed? "Well, have a good night."

"Ditto." *Please God, don't let me fall. Don't let me....* Floyd stopped him short, and he reached out, finding the house. *Okay. Left. Follow the house to the left.*

Floyd stopped him again at the steps, which he felt with his foot. *Okay, railing. Oops.* They were facing the railing. "Steps, Floyd." Floyd got that one six out of ten, and this time it worked, Floyd squaring him up with the stairs by leading him in a half arc.

Thank God.

"Hey. You made it. Come on in, y'all." His hand was placed on Stoney's warm arm, and he was moving again, going into a toasty room that smelled of… "Chili dogs?"

"Quartz had a craving."

"You can also have what Geoff is serving in the main dining room," Quartz said, sounding very serious. "Daddy will send me for it if you want."

"God no. Chili dogs are proof there is a God and He loves us. Are there chips too?"

"Yep. And coleslaw. Geoff and Uncle Ford are all weird about veggies at every meal."

Both Quartz and Stoney groaned in unison.

"Potatoes are a vegetable." Bleu reached out when Stoney stopped, touching the back of a chair.

"That's what I say. Let me take your coat."

"Does your dog need water?" Quartz asked.

"He could use some, I bet. How can it be snowing and dry as a bone?" He pulled out the old joke, because that was something they could commiserate over, New Mexico and Colorado, even if the Texan in him didn't get it.

"I know, right? Come on, pup. I have some cookies in here too."

Floyd's nails clicked on the floor. He never panicked when Floyd left him here. This was a good place.

"Come on, let's get you settled. You sure chili dogs are cool? Sometimes we just like to be… well, not fancy."

"If you promise not to stress if I spill on my shirt."

"Hell, buddy, I do that and I can see." That was Doogie, the sound of him pulling back his chair loud. His footsteps must have been lost in Floyd's and Stoney's.

"Hey, man. How goes it?"

"Good. Good. Ford playing host tonight?"

"Yep. Tomorrow's my turn."

"Fun." Doogie cackled. "Better you than me."

Stoney snorted. "You know I love the guests. Some days I just need to have chili dogs."

"I'm all over it." Doogie cleared his throat like he always did before he spoke to Bleu. "Hey, Bleu. Didn't expect to see you up for ski week."

He almost blurted out the surprise, but he caught himself just in time. "Ford invited me. I'm going to try skiing, have a few snowball fights, and relax for a little bit. Let the clay dry off my hands."

"Oh, cool." Doogie made him laugh, because that was it. He lost interest.

"I like to ski," Quartz said.

"Do you?" Of course Quartz would. He was a mountain kid. "Have you been doing it your whole life?"

"No. Just since I was three." Only a tween could sound so offended.

"I haven't learned how yet."

"Well, no. You're blind. What if you hit a tree?"

"Quartz!" Doogie sounded all offended. "You can't ask things like that."

"Why not?"

"Because it's… damn Sam."

Bleu shook his head, chuckling softly. "It's cool. Better to ask and find out, right? I'm going to have someone teach me. There are people that are trained to help guide blind skiers."

"Really? Like for real? Daddy! Daddy, did you know this? I want to do this. I want to be a guide."

Stoney's laugh was warm with pleasure. "Sure, son. Let's research how to get you the training you need."

"Cool! I could help people."

"You could. Your drink is at twelve, Bleu." Stoney was moving around.

"Thank you. What am I drinking?"

"Oh! I got iced tea, but would you rather have coffee or something else warm?"

"Iced tea goes great with chili dogs." He was just tickled Stoney allowed him to come eat.

"Thank goodness." Stoney laughed right out loud. "I get to know someone a little, and I think I know what they want."

"That's your job, isn't it, man?" To ascertain what people needed. Ooh. Ascertain. Ten-cent word. Go him.

"I guess? It's what I do." Stoney set the best-smelling plate in front of him. "There are onions, mustard, ketchup, and relish because Ford taught my son how to eat like someone not from Texas."

"Oh good Lord and butter…."

They started laughing together, and then Doogie joined them.

"What's so funny?" Quartz asked, which just set them off harder.

The door opened and closed, the smell of woodsmoke strong. "Did I miss something?"

That was Stoney's best wrangler, Tanner.

"They think chili dogs are funny."

"Ooh. Weenies. Is there enough for me too?"

"You know it, buddy. You know Bleu."

"I do." Tanner pressed a hand to his shoulder. "Glad you're here."

"Hey, Tanner. Did you have a good Christmas?"

"I did. It surprised me, because my girl dumped me at Thanksgiving." Tanner was chuckling, so clearly it wasn't a horror.

"Oh man. I'm sorry. I mean, I get it. I moved out of Dan's in November." It hadn't been sad, though. It had been liberating.

"Aw, man, that sucks. Did you find out his people were scary Oklahoma, uh, devout folks?"

"I found out he was allergic to Floyd. More importantly, I found out that I was… bored."

"Oh, I'm not sure if that's better or worse." Tanner hooted. "Her folks kicked me out. Her daddy didn't even bother to offer me a check or nothin'."

"Wow. Impressive. 'Twas the season." He found his iced tea and drank deep.

"Well, I didn't have to get any of them Christmas presents."

"Hand me the mustard, Quartz?" Doogie asked.

No one wanted to know if he was okay, or if he needed help.

"You want relish too?"

"God no. Freak of Nature Boy."

"Uncle Ford says relish is love." Quartz didn't sound worried at all.

"Your Uncle Ford also says that your daddy is pretty, little man. I can't trust his word."

Bleu began to chuckle around his hot dog. Oh man.

"He's not?" Now Quartz was all exaggerated surprise. Sarcasm, thy name was an almost teenager.

"Bleu, back me up here."

He opened his eyes comically wide, staring toward where he hoped Stoney was sitting. "He's the finest thing I've ever seen!"

Stoney chortled, and this time Quartz joined in. God, this was fun.

And chili dogs with relish? Not bad. Not bad at all.

Chapter Four

RYAN had put on a clean shirt for supper, mainly because he didn't want to upset Ford, who could be a snazzy dresser. It certainly wasn't for Bleu, especially since the man wasn't coming to supper. Or seeing Ryan even if he did.

Not that he was let down or anything.

There were about a dozen men in the dining room, the main communal table set with heavy stoneware, no delicate china here.

"Hey! Did you want a table to yourself or did you want to join us all at the big table?" Ford grabbed his hand and shook it.

"I'll sit at the main table, absolutely." He had to admit, Ford looked happy and totally at home here, wearing a pressed button-down and Wranglers, gorgeous ostrich boots.

"That's the best choice." Ford guided him to a chair next to a burly man with a shock of white-blond hair, and across from the guy who was here with Bleu.

"This is Sam Johnson. He's up from Austin. He owns a design company. And this is Dan Klah—he's in fine art."

"Hey." He nodded at Dan and then shook Sam's hand. "Ryan Shields. I'm from Vail for the time being."

"Nice to meet you. I've seen you on the slopes. Impressive."

"Thanks." Business he understood, and skiing and snowboarding was business. "It's what I'm good at."

Sam was adorable—tow-headed and sweet, young and clearly interested.

Dan, on the other hand, watched him intently, as if trying to figure him out.

"Bleu didn't come to supper?" Ryan asked, just to see what Dan would say.

"Hmm? No. He's staying in tonight. He wasn't well."

Ryan tried to school his face. Huh. Bleu wasn't talking to this guy already?

"Oh no! That's awful. Your first night here too. Maybe it's the altitude?" Sam seemed so sincere.

"He lives in Santa Fe," Dan said. "I think he just didn't want to be in a dining room."

Wait. Mr. I Can Do It was scared to eat? He'd eaten with Bleu for five years—in restaurants and at home, in the cafeteria and in bars. He had always been so easy in his skin.

Maybe that was why he was going to the family area instead of here….

Double huh.

Geoff's assistant, Tiny, started bringing out bowls of stew in his huge hands. The stuff smelled like heaven, and his mouth actually watered. "Thanks, Tiny."

"You're welcome. I'll bring cornbread shortly."

"Smells amazing," Dan said. "I love the food here."

He wanted to ask why Dan wasn't eating it with his hubby, but he bit it back. Maybe he was just bitter that his relationship hadn't worked out with Phil so he had no one to show off to the ex.

"Have you both been here before?" Sam asked. "This is my first time."

"Yeah. I come back every chance I get." Ryan smiled for Sam, knowing how hard it was to be new, and apparently alone.

Sam blushed for him, grinning back, the expression going eager.

He'd have to be careful, because he wasn't looking to hook up, but he could always use more friends. "So, what do you do in Texas, Sam?"

"Commercial art—you know, album covers, book covers, advertising, packaging, websites." Sam smiled at Tiny as he offered a piece of cornbread. "Please, thank you, sir."

Tiny gave the guy a slow once-over. "You're welcome."

Oh, look at that little shiver. Tiny was something else, huge and tattooed, with long, silky black hair pulled back in a tail and a beaded, braided beard. He would probably turn Sam inside out.

Ryan was jealous.

He turned to smile at Dan, who chuckled. "So you knew Bleu in college, he said? Hopefully you two can carve out time to catch up this week."

"Oh, yeah. Uh, sure. We could catch up." He didn't roll his eyes.

"I'd love to hear stories about when he was just a kid. I can imagine he was adorable."

"He was a voracious learner and a great debater." He chuckled. "Adorable? Maybe."

Bleu had been wild, had been eager to try everything, had been utterly ready to play. Just like him, come down to it.

They'd hurt each other good, but they'd loved like crazy too.

"A debater? Really? How interesting. I don't know that I've heard him have an opinion on anything but what to charge for his work."

He blinked. Surely Bleu hadn't changed that much. "Did he have a terrible accident or something?"

"Not that I know of, no. I mean, he does have his moments, but usually he's fairly graceful."

"Oh. I guess he just used to be more… outgoing."

"He's very focused on his work these days. Between commissions and his original pieces, he's quite in demand. Our job is to keep him focused."

"Our?" Sam raised his brows. "Like, more than one of you?"

"Me and his agent, Rob. We handle him together."

"Ah."

Handle. Lord have mercy, this guy was a piece of work.

"I employ ten artists for my design company, so I get that. Managing creative people is a… well, an art form." Sam looked happy to be in on the conversation.

Ryan snorted. "My manager says it's like herding cats. I am not a cat."

"No? More like a sled dog?"

He looked at Dan, eyes narrowing. Well, hello snarky. "Arooo."

Sam chuckled softly. "Very nice. I have bassets at home. I know from howling."

"Oh, I love hounds." He did. He'd had a bloodhound when he was a kid. "All that personality."

"And drool. There's some drool involved."

"Always."

Dan shuddered. "Hair. Dogs are so hairy. Makes me sneeze. I'm just not a fan."

Wait. Wait a minute. Bleu had a Seeing Eye dog. Was this guy the biggest asshole on earth or what? He shook his head. "That must suck, what with Bleu's Seeing Eye dog."

"God yes. Floyd sheds everywhere."

Sam was looking back and forth at them now, so Ryan put on a smile. "The stew is amazing."

"Isn't it? I'm loving the cornbread. I wonder if there will be more." Uh-huh. Sam was wondering if there would be Tiny.

"I bet there will. We're a bunch of hungry guys." The whole platter of cornbread was gone.

Sure enough, Tiny came out about two minutes later, bearing cornbread and crescent rolls too.

One platter was left on one end of the table, and then the second platter was offered to Sam.

"Thank you." Sam took one of each.

"You're welcome, honey." Tiny's voice was deep, rumbly, and really, really inviting. To Sam.

Sam reached in his wallet, pulled out a business card. "I'm in cabin five."

"Are you now?" Tiny winked before placing the tray in front of them to head back to the kitchen.

"It's worth a try, right, guys?"

"You know it, man. I can tell you Tiny is a nice guy as well as a hot guy." Ryan clapped Sam on the back.

"Thanks. I want to take my chances."

Dan nodded sagely. "I say go for it. Life is short."

"Exactly." Okay. That was a totally reasonable response. He clinked his glass of tea against Sam's beer bottle. "Go you."

Sam's grin was wicked, wild.

Ford came over to pull out a chair next to them. "All right, why are you all grinning like fools?"

"Sam here is coming on to Tiny."

Sam flushed deep, but he laughed, and Ford hooted. "He's something, our Tiny."

"Yessir."

"Oh, Lord love a Texan." Ford leaned against his shoulder, casual and relaxed. No stress.

Ryan was the one to laugh out loud this time. "You do."

"I do. I apparently have a long-term craving for the cowboy type."

"I get you." He nodded firmly. Not that cowboy was his thing, really. Texan? Oh, yeah. He had been known to get all over that.

He waited for Dan to agree too, but he didn't say a word. This man was strange as hell.

He raised a brow at Ford, who shrugged. God, was Bleu safe? Was he okay?

"So where's Stoney tonight?"

"In the family part of the house. The wranglers and Quartz really prefer to eat in the old dining room, which is like it was when I grew up."

"Ah, nice and casual, hmm?" So, no meetings with the owners. Just dinner with the working class. What the hell was going on with Bleu and this Dan guy? What?

It sounded like Bleu, though. Having the casual supper instead of the more formal.

He got it. He did. Luckily, nothing at the Leaning N this week was going to be fine dining but the Ski Weekend party.

And this stew was heavenly, *and* he'd been the one to request it. He crumbled more cornbread into it, then grabbed a roll to dip. He did love bread in and with his stew.

He yammered with Ford about the snowpack, about the best coffee in Aspen, about the amazing belt buckle Stoney had made for him.

Dan watched him carefully, which was a little unnerving, so he didn't linger over coffee and dessert. He asked Tiny to wrap up his apple pie for him.

"Here you go, Ryan. You call the kitchen if you want ice cream for it later."

"Thanks, guys. I'll see you in the morning sometime." Maybe he'd have breakfast in the kitchen with Geoff.

"Night!" Sam waved, so Ryan winked.

"Good luck," he said before heading out. He started for his cabin, which was still only his for the time being. On the way past the family wing of the house, he glanced over, looking through a window where light glowed.

Bleu was sitting there, half of a chili dog stuck to his cheek, laughing his ass off with Stoney and a couple of the drovers.

Ryan paused, blinking. This was the man he knew, not the one Dan had described.

Stoney's son stood there, eyes wide, and then he began to laugh too, like he wasn't sure he ought to.

Oh, Lord. Bleu was doing that shocking blind guy thing. How many times had he seen that? Bleu making fun of himself to make someone else feel more relaxed?

A lot. Some of the time with him. Ryan smiled, feeling kinda interlopery. He should move on.

He should, but he had to admit, it felt good, that goofy grin, how he could see the man he'd fallen in love with, so long ago.

Not that he was still in love. He just—Bleu was like whiskey, burning him to the ground.

He didn't need that shit. He didn't want to burn. He wanted a lover who…. Hell, he didn't know. He wanted a lover, he guessed. Not a business thing like Phil. Someone who was into him, all the way.

Ryan took his pie back to his cabin. He would eat it in bed. In his underwear, blaring AC/DC. So there.

Fuck, please let this week be over. Soon.

Chapter Five

BLEU was up and out before Dan even twitched, heading out to walk Floyd and then find the kitchen. He wanted to make snowballs and a snowman. He wanted bacon. He needed coffee.

He grinned a little because it was snowing again, fat, wet flakes that hit him like tiny snowballs themselves.

He could smell bread and hear warm laughter, and it drew him right up to the kitchen door. "Hello?"

"Hey!" That was Geoff, opening the door so a warm flush of yeasty air hit him. "Come on in! You need an arm?"

"Please. Am I bothering?" *Is there coffee?*

"Not one bit. I have everything you need to warm up." Geoff came down opposite Floyd and let him hold on up the stairs.

"Oh, good. I was up and looking for trouble."

"Already? You're early."

"I know!" He had to laugh, but it was true. He loved being out here, somewhere he could explore.

"You want coffee?" Geoff was still chuckling with him.

"God, please. Yes. I'd love one."

"Cream and sugar or Reese's creamer?"

"Ooh. Reese's, please. I love peanut butter. Love it." He found a chair and pulled it out to sit. "This one okay?"

"Perfect. Here you go." Geoff set a cup in front of him and, unselfconsciously, took his hand and put it on the handle.

"Thank you." He brought the cup up to his mouth, inhaling to test the heat. Oh, that smelled like heaven.

"No problem. I'm kinda still making bread, but if you're hungry, I can whip something up."

"No. No, this is fine. I wanted"—*company*—"to visit."

"Coolios." Geoff hummed, and the scrape of a chair sounded. "I can sit a minute. Yay!"

"I'm not bothering you, am I? It's still snowing. I can't believe how deep it is." The Texan in him was still losing his mind.

"Not a bit. It's just so high up here, but I bet the ski folks are tickled." Geoff sipped his coffee, which probably wouldn't make a sound to anyone else.

"I bet. Do you ski?" He was going to try. He couldn't wait.

"Me? God no. I started to learn when I was five. Broke my kneecap hitting a tree."

"Oh. Oh, ow. That sounds awful!" He'd broken… well, quite a few bones, honestly. Sometimes he fell.

"It kinda made me not want to again. I'm a wicked tuber, though." Geoff snort-laughed. "Not a potato. Inner-tubing."

"Inner… on the snow?" Oh. Oh, that sounded so fun.

"Yes! OMG, we should go. I have a five-man inner tube. We can do it together. Quartz loves it."

"Yes. Yes, please. Please. I want to." He nodded eagerly. "I've been tubing on the river. I loved that. I went river rafting in Taos too." That had scared Dan to death.

"Oh, I love that. My sister did rafting guide stuff with Quartz's mom in the summers."

"Hey, Geoff. Rumor is you have coffee." The voice was like whiskey over gravel. Damn. Ryan.

"I do!" Geoff's chair scraped back. "Remind me, Ryan?"

"He drinks it black." The words escaped him.

"Right." Geoff didn't even question it.

"You mind, Bleu?" Ryan asked softly.

"Have a seat. It smells good in here, doesn't it?" He could be a decent guy, see? Cool.

"It does. I love fresh bread."

"I want to make breakfast sandwiches for the main dining room. Is it okay to test them on you guys?" Geoff asked.

"Sounds amazing. What's in a breakfast sandwich?"

"We haff options," Geoff said with some weird accent no one could ever figure out. "Sausage, egg, and cheese; bacon, egg, and cheese; tofu scramble; or veggie frittata patties."

"Bacon, egg, and cheese for me, please." That sounded great. He was careful to be still, to focus on his coffee.

"Me too." Ryan made a happy noise. "I love a breakfast sandwich."

He'd want the sausage, back in their day, but Bleu thought Ryan was a professional athlete these days. Was bacon better for you than sausage? If Ryan was that worried, he would have gone for frittata, right? Or was that too much carb?

The door opened, cold air pouring in for a moment. "Woo! It is snowing like crazy!" That was Stoney, laughing and slapping his hat against his jeans, from the sound of it.

"It snowed on me!" He had to laugh. "Did you know there is snow tubing? Geoff's going to take me! Can someone spare a few minutes to make a snowman with me?"

"I bet Quartz would be happy to, and Sam said he wanted to. He's a Texan like us."

"You'll like him, Bleu. He's a nice kid," Ryan said.

"Cool. I like Texans, even though I'm a New Mexican now." He'd basically embraced his inner Santa Fean.

"Yeah. Me too," Stoney said. "Well, Coloradan. But I love my life."

"All the Californians are moving to Texas. We have to go somewhere."

"Yep." Stoney sat, so he must have been fixing coffee. "Y'all are up early."

"Am I? I know I beat Dan up." He touched his watch, and it said, "Seven forty-five." "Wow."

"I was ready to get out in the snow," Ryan said. "It's epic out there."

He wanted to go play too. He was going to learn how to ski. He wouldn't say that out loud, because damn, who wanted to talk about learning how to ski with a champion?

Ryan could do it all, and his one major sadness with Ryan was he would never get to see Ryan ski or snowboard.

He imagined it was like hard, fast sex, really going for it hammer and tongs. That, he did know. With Ryan.

Okay. Okay, no thinking about hard and fast anything. Last thing on earth he needed was to get wood here, now.

"Do you want to have breakfast here, boss, or are you going to eat with the guests?"

"I'm going to eat in here. I got to check the horses, and then I'm heading out on the snowmobile to look at the back pasture. I want to give it a look-see."

"Something weird?" Geoff asked.

"Nah. Just a lot of snow. We had some late calves, and I want to check on everyone."

"In other words, he wants to get out and play." Ford's voice was filled with warmth, humor, love. "Hey, baby." There was the distinct sound of a pecked kiss. They were adorable.

"Hey, mister. Coffee?"

"Please."

That was what he'd thought he wanted, what he'd had with Dan. It had bored him to death.

Geoff placed a plate in front of him. "Bread is still warm. Sandwich and fruit."

He reached out, tracing the edge of the plate. He felt a warmth on his arm, then heard, "Sandwich is in halves at nine, fruit is at three."

"Thank you." That shouldn't make him shivery. Not one bit. It made him think of so many intimate meals with Ryan, though, so many naked times. *Stop it. Be good. Stop it right now.*

He reached for his sandwich, needing to do something, anything. Thank God for having something to do with his mouth.

Was Ryan looking at him? Watching him? Wanting him?

"So, Ryan, are you gonna hit the slopes?" Ford asked.

"Yeah, I think I am. It's too good to pass up."

"Tanner's running a group to the lifts in an hour. You're welcome to ride with."

"Yeah? Thanks, Ford. Does your Dan ski, Bleu?"

"He goes up once or twice a year with clients, yeah." At least that was what he thought. Who knew? Dan was cagey.

"Cool. You ever gonna try it?" Ryan didn't sound ironic or mean. Just curious.

"Yeah. Yeah, I totally am. I want to try everything." He loved finding out new things.

"Very cool. Try tubing with Geoff first. It will really give you a feel for how cold it is up there, and how fast you're going." Stoney didn't sound worried at all. "Then we'll go snowmobiling."

"Yeah? Y'all rock. Don't tell Dan. He'll be all weird."

"Worries too much, does he?" Ryan chuckled. "I'm surprised you haven't bopped him on the nose."

"He's not the type." He had to grin, though, because he'd thought about it, once or twice, when they were still together.

"What type is he?" Now Ryan was sounding serious. And a little mad.

"Uh… classy, I guess. High dollar." Not like him. He was a talented, happy, wealthy goddamn redneck.

"Oh." Ryan relaxed, and he could literally feel it. What the heck?

He itched to reach out, touch Ryan's face and look. He actually reached out before he realized what he was doing and yanked his hand back, knocking over his coffee and upending his plate.

"Whoops!" Geoff was there with a towel, helping him mop up. "Let me get you more coffee, huh? Sandwich in five."

"You okay?" Ryan asked.

"I—I'm going to go. I'm sorry, Geoff. I don't need another sandwich." He grabbed for Floyd's harness, his cheeks flaming. *Way to show how competent you are to the ex, Bleu.*

He made it to the door, then stopped at the stairs, worried he would splat on his face in the snow.

"Hey." Ryan was right there, hand warm on his arm again. "No one is upset. It was an accident. I get it if you want to go, but don't run off on my account, huh?" Gently but firmly, Ryan steered him and Floyd in a circle.

"I just… I haven't done that in a long time." No wonder Dan didn't want to eat in the dining room with him. He was still a bit of a disaster.

"Is it me? The main dining room is about to open. I can head over there and have my second cup of coffee."

"No. I mean, I…." He stopped, forced himself to relax and let his tension out with a laugh. He wasn't a kid anymore; he could do this. Brutal honesty, right? "You still make me stupid. I wanted to look at you, and I don't have the right to anymore."

"Anytime you want to, Bleu. I'm not as much of an asshole as I was. I hope."

"None of us are." He reached up, lips parting as he let himself explore. There was a new scar next to Ryan's lip and there were laugh lines now, but the sharp cheekbones were the same, and so was the long nose. The bump at the bridge was more pronounced.

"I broke it again," Ryan admitted when Bleu lingered.

"How?" Oh, Ryan's hair was long now, like his.

"I face-planted on a jump. Came off the rail, landed too far forward, and boom. Broke my helmet, broke my nose." Ryan chuckled, the sound warm.

"Damn, baby."

"What on earth are you doing out here in the snow without a coat?" Dan's voice shocked the hell out of him.

"Did I forget my coat?" He damn near slipped off the steps, he jumped so hard. Floyd pulled him back to safety. "I was just getting coffee."

"Don't you snarl at him," Ryan snapped. "His coat is inside."

"Well, you've made a mess of yourself, I can tell. You're covered in coffee. You didn't burn yourself, did you?"

"No. No." *God.* "I'm going to change."

"Would you like me to bring you a plate of breakfast? I'm going to eat in the dining room."

"No, thank you. I'm going to make snowmen with Quartz. I'll change."

"Bleu… think of your hands."

"Uh-huh." He knew, but he could live with a little arthritis for an afternoon of play.

"Well, you holler if you need me, huh?" Dan sighed, but Bleu knew it was fond. He could tell.

"I will."

Dan trudged off, his boots cracking the snow crust.

"Is he abusing you, babe?" Ryan asked it baldly.

"Dan? Dan couldn't hurt a spider. He's just…." *Worried about appearances and about mess and about illness and about everything.* "He's just particular, and I'm not."

"Particular, huh. You don't even eat together."

"No, it makes him uncomfortable." For obvious reasons, he guessed. "You should remember that. You worried about having to take care of a blind man."

That put some steel in him, let him think again, remember that he wasn't helpless. He lived on his own. He was okay.

"I did." Ryan stepped back, letting him go. "I'll get your coat."

"No worries. I'll get it on the way back. I have to de-funkify myself." See him, see him be a reasonable guy, be calm and good-natured when what he wanted was to tackle Ryan.

"You okay to get to your cabin?"

"Floyd knows the way now."

"Hey! Here's your coat, Bleu, and I wrapped you up another sandwich." Geoff saved him from utter stupidity.

"Thank you. Can you tell Stoney—" *What? What, stand here in front of your "I don't want to be saddled with Bleu" ex and ask whether the twelve-year-old could come out to play with him? Christ.* "—to have fun on the snowmobile. I'll see y'all later."

"I'll tell him." Geoff pressed a kiss to his cheek before pushing a bag into his free hand.

"Thanks. Come on, Floyd." Floyd took him down the steps without killing either of them, and they blundered off through the snow. God, he was a fool. "Please, God," he whispered. "Let me get to the cabin without falling or something. Let me seem like I'm not an idiot."

It was the little victories in life, and this one worked. Floyd led him right to the correct door. He smelled Dan's cologne when he stepped inside.

Bleu inhaled deep, the scent comforting, gentle, classy. "Why couldn't I be in love with you, honey?"

He shook his head, letting Floyd go to his bed in the corner before devouring the sandwich Geoff had sent. Might as well before he changed. Oh, yum.

Bleu stripped his shirt off and found an old, soft T-shirt and a cozy sweatshirt. There. Better. Now, he needed long johns under his jeans, right? Denim was the death fabric in snow. He'd learned that in Santa Fe.

He was lacing his hikers back on when a soft knock sounded at his door.

"Hello? Come in."

"Mr. Bleu? Daddy said I could come ask if you wanted to play. I love snowmen." Quartz slipped in, and Floyd's tail began to thump on the floor. Quartz had a real way with animals.

"Yeah? You do? I want to make some, so bad."

"I totally do! Oh my gosh, no one ever makes them with me but Geoff, and he's so busy today making stuff for when all the skiers get here."

"Let's go, then. We'll make a bunch." God knew, he was sort of incredibly qualified, right?

"Do you need help finding anything? Gloves and stuff? Geoff says you're going tubing tomorrow. He says he has a fartbag for you."

"A what?" His gloves were in his coat.

"A fartbag. That's what Geoff calls a one-piece snowsuit."

"Oh." He started chuckling, tickled pink. "Dude. I like that. Where's the best place to do this snowman thing?"

"I'll take you. There's a great place in the yard where there's no horse poop and not much dog poop. I'll clean that up real fast."

"Fair enough. Let's make this happen. What kind of snowmen do you want?"

"I—is it gonna be weird if I say like Calvin and Hobbes? I read Daddy's books. They were all like horror ones. Dinosaurs eating people. Giant snow heads eating little snow people."

He loved how Quartz never assumed he knew what things looked like. Quartz was so good at explaining.

"Oh, we can totally do that. Completely."

"We can!" Quartz whooped. "Okay. You need a hat too. Your head will get all wet."

"Right. Do you see one, man? It's got a poof on top."

"I do! Here it is." Quartz handed it to him.

"Let's do this." He fastened his coat and took Quartz's arm. "Lead the way."

This was way more fun than staying in and pouting.

Chapter Six

RYAN decided not to go skiing up at the slopes. He needed more workout than fun, so after he suited up at his cabin, he headed out to ask Ford about cross-country skis.

He got hooked up and headed out into the forest to get his shit together. God, he'd damn near lost it when Bleu had touched him, looked at him. He was still… even after all this time and that disastrous relationship with Phil, he wanted Bleu.

He pushed up a hill so he could coast down the other side. Yeah, that was working muscles he might have forgotten he had. God, he needed to do this more often. Get out and work on stamina instead of speed.

Not that he was ever competing again. Ever. But he needed to remember there was more to life than downhilling and shit.

God, it was beautiful up here. Quiet. Still. There were tracks everywhere. Deer. Birds and rabbits. Maybe a big cat, if he wasn't mistaken.

He leaned against a tree, sucking water and taking a rest. He was going to have to come up again, maybe tomorrow.

Maybe the day after. His muscles would need rest. He checked his watch. Shit, he had almost an hour's ski back to the ranch.

He turned his music on for the ski back, letting the tracks drive him down the mountain. He coasted some of the way, which was good, tucked down with his poles up. Then he found places where the still-falling snow was so powdery he almost sank, and he had to power through.

When he broke through the trees, he stopped short, trying to understand what he was looking at.

Monsters.

Dozens of snow monsters.

He chuckled, and that became a full-on, if breathless, laugh. Oh, look at that. There was a minotaur chasing a whole herd of mini cows. A giant yeti. A tiny set of snowmen running in terror from a giant rolling boulder….

Quartz.

There was Quartz in snow, directing the whole shebang. He looked like a mini dictator, and Bleu was working like one of Santa's elves, feverishly sculpting. Good Lord.

He pulled out his phone and snapped pictures furiously. That was the neatest thing he'd ever seen. The whole thing should be on TV or something, but he would immortalize it.

As he got closer, he frowned. Bleu was kneeling in the snow, and he didn't have gloves on at all.

Had they been out here all morning? Seriously?

"Hey, there! See our army? Isn't it amazing?" Quartz looked on top of the world.

"It's amazing." He clicked out of the skis. "I mean really. I took so many pictures. Has anyone else seen it?"

"I don't think so. When we're done, I'll get Uncle Ford and Daddy."

He moved closer to Quartz. "I think Bleu is about to freeze, kiddo. He can't see what color his hands are, but we can."

"Oh. Should I go get them now? Will you stay with him?"

"I will. Thanks, Quartz. Bleu is very happy, I can tell, but he needs a rest." He didn't touch, because Geoff had warned him Quartz had to be the one to initiate that, but he left no doubt he was proud and pleased.

"Thank you!" Quartz ran off, and he went right to Bleu.

"Honey, you have to stop. Your poor hands."

"Huh?" God, some things never changed.

"You took your gloves off. If you lose a finger or two to frostbite, no one will forgive you." He took those cold as hell fingers in his.

"I was…." Bleu's teeth began to chatter. "When did it get cold?"

He laughed. "It's been cold. Come on, let's get you inside."

He led Bleu toward the kitchen. There would be food and cocoa and warmth there. "Where's Floyd?" he asked, looking around for the dog.

"Pouting somewhere. I wouldn't come with him when he nudged."

"Floyd's in the kitchen, Mr. Bleu. I brought them to see!"

"Thanks, Quartz. I'm gonna warm up, okay?" Bleu shook like an Aspen leaf.

"Oh my God. Ford, look at this." Stoney was just hooting.

"It's fabulous. Get him in the house, Shields."

"I'm on it." He hustled Bleu into the house. "Geoff?"

"He's in the pantry." Tiny turned to look at them. "Here. There's a fire in the family room. I'll bring some towels for his hands. We have to warm them up slower than the rest of him. Get his boots off, and I'll bring dry socks."

"I'm okay…." Bleu held on to him, refusing to let him go.

"I got you, babe. I swear." He took Bleu right into the family room to plop him in a platform rocker style chair. He could shove the whole thing across to the fire where he could put Bleu's feet up.

"Socks," Tiny said, handing him a pair of the biggest, fuzziest slipper-socks he'd ever seen. They had cats on them.

"What kind of cat do you have, Tiny?"

"A big fat Persian."

"Is he a Texan?"

Tiny blushed, but that grin said volumes. "Well, no, but I have recently gotten into one of those."

He cackled, and Bleu frowned. "What did I miss?"

"I'll tell you, babe." Before he put the socks on Bleu, he took off the soaked boots, socks, and jeans. "Long johns. I approve."

"Thanks."

Geoff appeared with pajama pants and a blanket. "Here we go. Be back with hot choccie in a flash. You want hot towels for the hands?"

"Please." Tiny had said warm. He figured those two would work it out. "Stand up a minute, babe?" Where the hell was Dan?

"Okay…." Bleu stood for him without question.

He slipped the new jammie pants on Bleu's feet one by one. "Okay, have a sit." He pushed on the socks once Bleu sat, then covered Bleu with the blanket. The shirt would have to go too—

"Here. A sweatshirt," Tiny said. "Warm towels."

"I feel so silly," Bleu said.

"You were having such a good time," Ryan murmured.

"We were."

God, those poor baby swollen hands. Ryan wrapped the big towel around them, and Bleu hissed. "I know. It will feel better soon. Do you have that arthritis lotion in your cabin?"

"Yeah. Always. You know."

He did. The autoimmune disease that ruined Bleu's eyes affected his joints too.

"Cool. We'll get that on you when you thaw out." Physical stress was Bleu's kryptonite. He could get sick in a heartbeat when he was overtaxed.

"Was Quartz pleased?" Those bright eyes moved constantly, searching for God knew what. Ryan remembered that, how Bleu could exhaust himself without even knowing it.

"He was like a general leading a charge. Hell, they're still out there looking, so I bet he's showing them every detail." He rubbed the towel gently over Bleu's arms. "It's amazing, babe."

"Thanks. It was fun. Did you have a good day?"

"I skied out a long way. It was good. I decided I needed time to myself, not a crowded slope." Selfish?

Yeah, probably, but half the time he never made it up the lift.

"You'll need to have a long bubble bath and a whiskey tonight."

"I will." He stopped himself from asking Bleu to join him. The man was married, for God's sake.

"Good. I remember that. You and your bubble baths." The expression on Bleu's face didn't hide a thing.

"Yeah? I still love them." He looked at his hands, which were moving on Bleu's skin now with no towel.

Geoff saved him. "Hot cocoa! And cookies to get the blood moving."

He wasn't sure whether to kiss Geoff or punch him in the face. Ryan settled on grateful. He wasn't an asshole. Ryan stood. "Thanks, man. That smells amazing, huh, Bleu?"

"It does. Cream and… peppermint?"

"Good nose." Geoff smiled down at Bleu and helped him wrap those swollen fingers around the hot mug.

"Thank you. I feel ridiculous."

"We've all lost track of time in the snow, honey. I need you all thawed so we can go tubing." Geoff patted Bleu's cheek. He was such a sweetie.

"Yeah. I want to learn how to do everything. Everything."

"I know! Oh, hey, Dan. Do you want chocolate?"

Ryan backed off when Dan came pelting in. "Bleu! Oh, you're so cold."

"I was out playing in the snow." Bleu's grin was pure evil.

Ryan snorted into the cup Geoff had handed him. Yeah. Those two had a weird thing, didn't they?

"Your hands!" Dan sighed. "I'll get your lotion."

"Don't stress it, man. I'm good. I had a ball. Did you see?"

"I did." Dan chuckled. "I need to go take pictures for your portfolio, you nut."

"Yep. A whole new media for me."

"Uh-huh. Stick to clay, dork." Dan rolled his eyes and then grinned at Ryan. "I used to threaten to keep him on a leash, but I don't bother anymore."

"No, I imagine that wouldn't work well."

At the word leash, Floyd padded out of the kitchen, nails clicking across the uncovered areas of hardwood. They all laughed, and Bleu reached down to rub the shepherd's ears. "Silly goober."

Bleu was so tactile, so happy to connect and laugh and touch, but he never once reached for Dan. Weird.

Ryan shook it off. It wasn't his place to judge, even if he wanted to just tell Dan to go away so he could bask in Bleu's happy glow. He was the ex.

Bleu was looking for him. He always felt that way. So weird. True, but weird.

Ryan sighed. "I'm gonna go get changed, guys. Bleu, you got this?"

"I do. Thanks."

"Bleu, you have on pajama pants with cartoons on them. You can't be wandering around with those."

"I won't. I'm going to the cabin and soak in the tub. Maybe a bubble bath. I wonder if they have any here…."

"We do." Stoney was back inside now. "Quartz, can you go get the wee packs of not flowery bath bubbles?"

"Yessir. Thank you, Bleu. They're the best snowmen ever!" Quartz really did sound so tickled.

"I had the best time, man. You totally rock my world."

Stoney grinned as Quartz ran off. “I swear, Bleu, he’s never going to forget this. You made him the happiest kid on earth.”

“Good. I had a ball.”

They were still laughing and chatting when Ryan left the room after a soft goodbye to Bleu. His muscles were aching and his ski boots were like lead. Time for a rest. Tiny handed him a sandwich on the way through the kitchen, making him laugh. Food was totally love.

Chapter Seven

"YOU are going to break your neck one of these days, you know?" Dan's voice was half-concern, half-laughter. "Tubing, freezing, what next?"

"Tomorrow there's going to be downhill skiing!" Bleu was finally going to feel what Ryan did.

"Oh God, tell me they got you a good instructor." Dan was more concerned now.

"They have to take training and shit. No worries." He wasn't scared, why should Dan be?

"I just want you to be safe," Dan murmured.

"I know." But it didn't matter. He wanted to be real; he wanted to play. He wanted to experience everything.

That was the crux between him and Dan. That was why they'd broken up. Safety.

"I know, hon. I love that about you, but it scares me."

"What are you going to do tonight? Is there a party?" The big unveiling was Saturday night, but the ranch had a bunch of different parties the entire week.

"I have no idea. I haven't checked the schedule."

"Me either," he teased. "We could play Twister."

"Oh, yeah, because I'm so graceful." Dan hooted. "The schedule is here."

"Tiddlywinks?" What the fuck were tiddlywinks anyway?

"What's gotten into you?" Dan squeezed his shoulders. "There's a gala in Aspen, a night ski at Sunlight Mountain, and a brisket supper and a movie here."

"Are you going to Aspen?" Dan loved to wear a tux.

"I think so. Do you mind?"

"Of course not! Go! Find a studly little skibunny to fuck into the floor."

"Bleu!" Dan started to laugh.

"Just remember to take condoms."

"I will. Even if you're awful."

"I am. I want you to be happy. I want you to be well-fucked and joyous."

"I do too." Dan kissed his cheek, which he'd felt coming, but it was still a surprise. "I think I'm going to shower, unless you need the bathroom?"

"Go for it. I'm going to walk Floyd and go see if someone wants to feed me."

"You could call," Dan said gently.

"I could. I'll bundle up. Maybe listen to the movie."

"Do you want me to call and make sure they have room at the table?"

"No." Did they find him a bother? He didn't think so. No one ever acted like it. "No, I'm fine, Dan."

"Okay, hon. I'm going to shower and dress. Have a good night."

"You too. Report back in the morning!" He laughed as Dan huffed, but he knew Dan would find someone. He knew it.

He would have the cabin to himself tonight. *Forrest Gump* time!

First, though, he'd take Floyd out, take a walk, and peek in at the kitchen, see if he could say hi.

He put his coat on and got Floyd leashed so he could do his business, then moved toward the main house.

Should he go in at the kitchen again? Geoff was always there, and he didn't seem to mind Bleu's company. At least he thought so. He didn't want to interfere with family time with Stoney and Ford, but he didn't want to be a bother to Geoff. If they needed him to go to the main dining room, he would.

Hell, he could even skip a meal. He'd been known to, when he was working.

"You lost, Bleu?"

"Huh?"

"You're heading a little left of the house, babe." Ryan put Bleu's hand on his arm.

"Oh. I think Floyd is mad at me for having so much fun without him."

"He would have turned you back, right?"

"Yeah. Yeah. Did you have a good day? Are you going to the big party in Aspen?"

"Nope. It's a fancy fundraiser. I am not allowed at those." Ryan laughed.

"Me either!" Although that wasn't true. He was welcome; he just didn't want to go.

"Well, you just have this spill threat. Me? I tell sponsors to go fuck themselves. Stairs."

They headed up, and warmth hit him. Oh, he loved that sensation.

"Hey, folks." That was Tiny, welcoming them in.

"Hello, Tiny. Are y'all busy?"

"No, sir. Hell, Geoff called off the brisket dinner. Everyone is up to that big gala. I hope you two like mac and cheese."

"Oh God. Please. I love cheese and noodles. I make it in the microwave all the time."

"Well, you ain't seen nothing like Geoff's baked stuff, then." Tiny laughed, a huge, booming sound.

"Here, babe. Sit down." Ryan tugged out a chair for him.

"Thank you." He settled down, keeping his hands in his lap.

"No problem." Ryan's chair scraped out too, and someone placed glasses on the table.

"Water," Tiny said. "Anyone want a hot or cold drink? Tea, Coke, coffee? Hot tea?"

"Can I have a Dr Pepper, please? Cherry, if you have it."

"We do. Stoney loves it." The pop of a can opening was followed by more ice in a glass.

"Thank you." God, he loved that bubbly, sweet, fake cherry smell.

"You're so welcome." Tiny joined them at the table, the chair creaking.

"So did you and the Texan get it on, Tiny man?" Ryan asked.

"What Texan? What did I miss?" Everybody knew everything.

"Sam. Remember? I told you that you should meet him."

"Little artist. Dan liked him."

"Yeah." Ryan chuckled. "Tiny was making with the wooing."

"He's a lovely man," Tiny rumbled.

"Rock on!" He was all about getting laid.

"Yeah. It rocked all sorts of things." Tiny snorted, and they all laughed.

"What did I miss?" Geoff said. "Oh! Yay. I made a lot of mac, and I was worried no one would eat it."

"I love macaroni. How was your day, Mr. Geoff?"

"It was crazy. I'm glad the big Aspen thing is tonight so I can put my feet up."

"I can take the food to my cabin, if you want. Dan's gone to the gala."

"Why would I want that?" Geoff sounded genuinely puzzled. "You guys are easy-peasy."

Oh, good. He wanted to be welcome and easy. "Thanks, Geoff."

"Why aren't you going to the gala?" Ryan asked.

"I'd totally be in Dan's way."

"So, he just left you here?" Ryan's voice rose a little.

"Yep. He needs to go have fun."

"Dan always likes the fancy," Geoff put in. "Bleu is a kitchen table kind of guy."

"You know it. He's a champagne guy, and I'm a…."

"Cherry Dr Pepper?" Geoff teased.

"You got it." Bleu nodded happily. Why was Ryan so darned upset about that? Maybe… maybe Ryan was jonesing on Dan? How weird would that be?

"Why are you frowning so hard, babe?" Ryan murmured.

"Am I?" He loved that, secretly, that babe. He also loved how Ryan helped him with his facial expressions. He had no idea sometimes.

"You are." Ryan touched the corner of his mouth. "Did you want to go? I'd take you."

"Go where?" This was perfect—good food, good company.

"To the gala. I mean, you never were one for formals, but I can see how it would hurt to be left behind."

"Oh, God no. I don't want to be stuck in a corner somewhere, listening to chatter and glassware."

"Okay, good. I really want that mac and cheese." Ryan's chuckle slid right up his spine.

"Uh-huh. It smells like cheesy heaven."

"Can I ask you a question, Mr. Bleu?" Tiny asked.

"Sure." He was easy.

"What do you do in your spare time? I think just sitting would be so boring…."

He chuckled. "I play a lot on my computer. I listen to audiobooks. If I have someone over, I play cards or games—I love checkers and cribbage."

"He's amazing at cribbage," Ryan said. "Like wicked good."

"I am. I watch a lot of movies too, go to the coffee shop and read. Normal stuff."

"That's really cool. I've never met someone who was blind before." Tiny wasn't being ugly at all, and Bleu loved when people asked real questions.

"I don't remember ever seeing, so I don't miss it." Sometimes he wanted to know what everyone else did, but he was basically okay. Not a burden.

Ryan's fingers curled around his, warm and comforting. Oh, he missed that, just the casual touching.

He let his fingers move, trace one finger after another, draw a circle at the fleshy part of Ryan's thumb.

Ryan hummed, the sound so familiar, so hot. This was such a mistake, but he loved those callused hands.

He remembered them on his body, unafraid to make his skin sing, to touch him deep and make him ache.

Sometimes the loneliness got bad.

"Babe, relax, huh?" Ryan smoothed out his forehead, pushing until the lines eased.

"Sorry. Sorry. I was getting maudlin." He chuckled, the mood lifting under Ryan's care.

"Maudlin? Why on earth for?" Geoff plopped something on the table in front of him, the smell of cheese heady. "Ta-da."

"Mmm… smells good."

"The ramekin is superhot, now. Take care."

"Okay." He slid his fingers over the table, the heat glowing from the dish before he touched it.

Wow. That had to be right out of the oven.

Another something landed on the table. "Salad. You have your choice of balsamic or zesty italian. Acid to cut the richness, huh?"

"I'm easy." He wanted the italian, but he didn't want to ask for help in front of Ryan more. He didn't want anyone to think he wasn't capable.

"Zesty, babe?" Ryan just went ahead and dressed his salad.

"Thank you. Yes." Ryan remembered. God, that shouldn't feel so good.

"Cool. There's garlic bread too. Want?"

"Always. There's no bad in bread, right?"

"Nope." Ryan put something just to the right of his hand. "Mac, salad, then bread."

"Thank you." Salads were always a surprise. Could be cheese, could be radish. Maybe tomato, possibly just a forkful of dressing. Life was a mystery sometimes.

The salad was kind of an italian chopped, with cheese and meat and yummy veggies. He dug in, eating happily, then focusing on the mac and gooey cheesiness. It had cooled just enough to gel back together, and God, it was good. Smokey, tender, perfectly melted.

"Mmm."

The room was silent except for the sounds of silverware. That showed the talent of the cook.

Ryan leaned in, lips near his ear. "I love to watch you eat, still."

His entire body went tight as hell. His heart began to race, and his cheeks felt hot. God, all this time he was spending with Ryan was killing him in the best way.

His cock was rock-hard, throbbing in his jeans.

He kept his head down, but he smiled. "Thanks."

God, he could smell Ryan. Right there. Rich and male, musk and soap. He closed his eyes and hummed, drawing it in.

"Babe, please. You have to stop this. It's not cool."

Ice water poured over him in a rush, and he stiffened. Floyd nudged his leg, worried, and he reached down to comfort and hide his face.

"I'm sorry," Ryan whispered, "but you're married. I'll back off too, I swear."

"What?" Married? Him? "What did you say?"

"I said married. I saw your engagement in the papers, and he's here with you…." Ryan trailed off, so his expression must have shown the gathering storm.

"So what…. You thought I'd come out and about to fuck around? Blind guy can't make it with his husband, so he's…. God, I've never cheated on anybody. Not ever in my whole life." He'd never told anybody he was married to Dan. No one.

"I—no. No, I just think I was pushing you. I shouldn't—"

"No. I'm not—" Helpless. Stupid. Someone who needed taking care of. Even though that was all Ryan had done. Helping him. Christ.

"Not what?" Ryan leaned into his space. "Not flirting right back at me?"

"No." Of course he'd been flirting. Ryan was fine to him. He grabbed at Floyd's harness. He wanted to go home, and since he couldn't do that, he wanted the cabin.

"Then what is it? Not what?" Ryan grabbed his arm. Where was everyone? Why wasn't someone saving his ass from himself?

"I'm not a cheater. I'm not an asshole." He was a good man. If he'd taken vows, he would never come on to another man.

Were Geoff and Tiny just watching this?

"No, your husband is. What kind of guy walks off and leaves you to go to supper or go to a gala?"

"The kind of guy that's not married to me."

"What?" Ryan stuttered a little. "Not married?"

"No." He pulled away. He wanted to go home. "Floyd. Come on."

The door out was behind him. Behind him.

Floyd was perfect, leading him to the door, then down the steps without killing anyone. So good.

Get to the cabin. Get to the cabin and close the door. God, Ryan thought he was.... Really? He'd never been a cheater. Not once. He was focused. No one had ever said he was fickle.

And who had told Ryan he was married? To Dan? That explained why Ryan had been all mad at Dan, but that also meant the asshole thought he was a perpetual victim.

Looked like things didn’t change. He still wanted Ryan. Ryan still felt sorry for him. He was still heading to sleep alone.

He was going to go for his ski lesson tomorrow, and then he was going to hang out until the unveiling Saturday. Then maybe he’d hire a car to take him home to Santa Fe. Leave Dan to do whatever.

Bleu was damned if he was going to be a burden on anyone.

Except maybe Floyd.

Chapter Eight

GOD, it was early.

Okay, it was only 8:00 a.m., but it was too early to be at the ski-out area on the special hill in Aspen, waiting for his client to show up. Ryan volunteered with a program where he taught people with physical disabilities to ski, and he wasn't going to let down his client, even if he'd drunk a little too heavily last night and couldn't remember to check the dude's name on the roster. Eh, that's what trainee volunteers were here to help with, right? Right.

He should have known better than to start something with Bleu, but the hot son of a bitch had been staring at him with an expression of pure need. How could anyone fight that? Anyone?

Especially when he didn't want to fight it.

But if he wasn't married, what the hell was Bleu doing with that guy?

Were they fuck buddies? Roommates? What?

Argh. He shook his head, then checked his watch. Two minutes. Was he getting stood up?

"Okay, Mr. Bridey. Just a few more steps."

"It's a hell of a challenge without Floyd."

Bleu. Oh hell no.

"Hey, Mr. Shields, I have your student for the day, Bleu Bridey."

Bleu stiffened, and Ryan sighed. "Hey, Bleu."

"Hey." Bleu looked totally confused for a second. "So, this is awkward. Can someone take me back to the ranch?"

"Sir? Mr. Stoney will be back at three o'clock…."

"Can you give us a minute, Tyler?" The kid wasn't at fault here. He was just a volunteer too.

"Of course. Sure." A volunteer and seventeen and terrified.

He turned to Bleu. "I had no idea you were my client, Bleu. I promise. I wouldn't do that to you." That was important, that Bleu didn't think Ryan was fucking him around.

"Of course you wouldn't." Bleu kept his head down. "Obviously I didn't know either. You've done your duty. You showed up. I'll go find somewhere to wait for my ride back."

"Wait." He didn't touch, but he did move to cut Bleu off. "Look, you want to learn to ski. I heard you talking about it. Not only am I really good at this, but I have to earn my volunteer hours, so you'd be helping me out."

He could see the emotions cross Bleu's face—eagerness and shame, curiosity and worry—and finally Bleu just shrugged. "You don't have to pretend that I'm helping. I just want to see what it feels like once, okay? I've always wondered."

"I'm not lying. I have to do damn near fifty more hours of volunteer service." He'd been hit with a great big fine for supposedly fixing his board during an event. He hadn't done it, but the board had decided against him, and this was how he was working it off. The thing was, he was damn good at teaching people with physical limitations, and he loved it. God knew he had experience and a shit-ton of respect for people willing to get out on skis. "So can we do this?" At Bleu's silent nod, he went on. "We'll get you used to the skis and the equipment. Then we'll do a few passes before we hit the slopes."

He wasn't sure what was safest for Bleu—leading the man down the hill or letting Bleu go in front and steering him from behind. They would figure it out after the start-and-stop training. That told him more about potential skiers than anything else.

"Yeah. Let's try this." Bleu sounded… diminished somehow? That wasn't going to work, not at all. Bleu wasn't married. That meant the man was fair game, and God knew he was interested.

He had some shit to make up for, old and new.

Good thing he was charming and a good teacher.

"Come on and suit up. You're not dressed for it." He took Bleu's hand and put it on his arm.

Bleu followed along, quiet, careful, and Ryan told himself to breathe. Bleu would relax. He loved to play, to learn new things. Ryan just needed Bleu to go with it.

They hit the locker room, where he helped Bleu change into a two-piece suit and boots. "Nice. You look like a pro."

Bleu flexed for him, posing playfully.

"Seriously. You're really fit. Now, there's gloves and a helmet, and you're gonna feel weird wearing the goggles, but you totally need them to protect your eyes."

"From what?" Bleu put the helmet on, then the gloves.

"Injury. I've found that blind people especially open their eyes and try so hard to see. You may not be able to use them like I do, but if you injured something, it could cost you a lot of time and money. You ready to try them?" He wanted Bleu comfortable with them on and off.

"I guess. Yeah. I don't want to be hurt."

"Okay, feel their weight." He walked Bleu through every piece of equipment there. They would do it again before they left the shed, and again on the bunny slope.

Bleu was a good student, even if he wrinkled his nose at the goggles. "How do you feel anything?"

"Trust me, you do. You feel a lot less with a visor helmet, but for serious downhill, that's a must." Bleu would get it.

He walked Bleu through stepping into the binding, and checked that he had the right fit. "We'll do this again out on the snow. Just remember to make sure they fit correctly. If not, you have too much snow on your boots, and they won't stay on."

"There's a lot of parts. No wonder no one wants to do this with me."

"You mean at home?" When Bleu nodded, he snorted. "You can find a volunteer almost anywhere. Just call the ski mountain. You ready to head out into the snow?" That would cheer Bleu right up.

"Sure. Let's do it." That was Bleu, always ready to try.

He took Bleu outside, and Ryan carried the skis. Bleu might brain someone. His ex was still too quiet, but the crunch of snow under his boots finally made him smile.

"You're going to love this, you know," he muttered.

"I'm not scared."

"Good." They headed out to the bunny slope, no lift needed. In fact, it was half-deserted, because for two hours the slope was for disabled folks instead of kids and beginners. "Okay, so now we put the skis down perpendicular to the slope. Can you feel the gravity pulling?"

"Yeah. Yeah. That I get." Bleu pointed down the hill, unerringly.

"Okay, so here's the ski, front and back of the binding." He showed Bleu all the steps, which had to be done by feel, and how to step into the downslope ski first.

Ryan started with the basics, and Bleu followed the steps like a champ. Way sooner than even he had expected, they were ready to start. "Okay, this slope kinda ends up taking you circular. It's not a lot of downhill. You know how to stop. I think you're gonna be good enough I can steer from behind, but I need you to listen and do anything I tell you."

"I can do that. I'm good at directions."

Yeah. Yeah, Bleu was. Bleu'd been following audible directions his entire life.

"I know. I'm seriously pleased at how quick you got all this. Okay, here we go."

They made it down without face-planting, which was a success, even if Bleu fell when he tried to stop.

Ryan whooped. "You did it! Remember what I told you about the latch on the binding when you fall?"

"Make sure the lever is down." Skis popped loose when you fell, if you went down hard enough. A skier had to know how to put them back on.

"Wanna go again?"

"Uh-huh. Please. Can we?" Look at that smile.

That was what he wanted. "We so can. Okay, now you learn how to get back up the bunny."

"All this learning." Bleu chuckled. "Show me."

They stayed out on the slopes the whole time, but when kids started whizzing by them, Ryan called a halt. "Come on and get a cookie and some hot chocolate. I'll text Stoney and tell him to fetch you and bring you back."

After a snack and a visit. Possibly a beer.

"Did I do okay?"

"You did amazing." He threw an arm around Bleu and smacked a kiss on his red cheek. "Okay, skis off over here."

"Right."

Bleu was going to be sore tonight, he'd bet. He wondered if he offered to massage those thighs what Bleu would say.

Probably no. He'd really upset the guy, and he couldn't say he didn't know why. He could be forgiven his assumption, but the idea that Bleu would cheat was definitely absurd.

Bleu was the most committed man he'd ever known.

He managed to get Bleu unwrapped and sat down, a cup of cocoa and a plate of cookies in front of him. The long pale hair was wild, coming out of his ponytail. Bleu was a little windburned, but the blue eyes were lit up and dancing.

"That was the best!"

"Better than tubing?"

"Yeah. That was fab, but I never got to steer. This I felt like I was doing. Although tubing was faster. That was cool."

"Yeah, speed can be great. You here for a few more days?" *Please let it be so.*

"I have to stay through the party Saturday night. I'm not booked for another few days after that, so I may hire a car to take me home later, if Stoney has a place for me."

"Yeah? Did you ride up with Dan?" He was being greedy, but he would love to ski again with Bleu.

"Yeah, I did. He was coming up anyway, so he volunteered."

"Ah. Well, we could go down to Sunlight Mountain and do another session. I could get you on a better hill there."

"You don't have to, Ryan. Thanks for the offer, though."

"I had a ball today." Bleu was slipping through his fingers already, now that they were off the slopes.

"Me too. It was… it was amazing. Thank you."

"You're welcome. I knew you could do it. You know… I can drive you back to the ranch. I have to go anyway." It wasn't like he'd texted the ranch yet, right?

"Do you want to? I mean, if you don't want to…."

"Don't, Bleu. I want to. Hell, let's go have a beer, have some food before we go back. I owe you an apology."

"I—" Those eyes moved back and forth, Bleu clearly thinking too hard. "Okay, but no place fancy, okay? I'm too tired for not spilling."

"Shit, I'm thinking a burger and fries."

"I like a burger."

"I knew that about you." He checked his phone real quick, because places in Aspen changed so quickly. CP's would work. "There's a good burger place a stone's throw away."

"Perfect. Do you remember that place in Boulder? The Sink?"

Did he remember? Fuck, he'd fallen in love watching Bleu lick his lips after eating the barbecue burger. "God yes. They had the best pizza too. I feel a little like I'm cheating on Beau Jo's to say it too. Remember that rafting trip to Idaho Springs?"

"I was good at rafting!" Good at it and fearless.

"I sucked at picking hotels. God, it was hot in there, and the stairs!"

"The asshole rednecks having a fight right outside our door."

"I know. You were super brave." Bleu had marched right out to the stairs that went up over their room and screamed. A lot.

That had totally gotten Bleu laid.

They both laughed, and he took Bleu's hand to take him to the changing room. Back to street clothes for supper.

"You're good at teaching, you know?"

"Yeah? I like it. I mean, I don't think I would be good at teaching dozens of tourists at a time, but this kind of instruction? It's super fulfilling." He meant it too. His life had changed a lot.

"Good. I'm still studio guy, more than anything."

"Yeah. You do all right, huh?"

"I do, believe it or not. I hit about two years after we graduated. I was doing miniatures for a production company, and this producer fell in love. With my work, not me. Although we're friends, still."

"That's too cool." Thank God they hadn't hooked up. He was seriously planning his attack on Bleu's heart. If he'd ever been worried Bleu needed a keeper, he wasn't now, and he got why Bleu had left him. No one wanted to be a burden, and to see how Bleu was with Dan made Ryan ashamed of how scared he'd been.

"Thank you. I was proud. Still am."

"I bet. I can't wait to see your statue. Geoff told me."

"It's a huge surprise. I hope it's right. Ford liked it."

"I'm sure it is, babe. I mean it. Your work was stunning years ago." It had to be better now.

"I have to find a new studio in Santa Fe. I'm still working from Dan's."

"Yeah?" Ryan frowned. "Are you living there?"

"Not anymore, no. I'm renting a little place near the Plaza. I'm trying to decide where I want to buy."

"Ah." His heart pounded a little. Bleu really was a free agent. He had no idea what that meant for him, but it gave him hope.

"I know. My folks say I ought to come home to Austin, but… I've been on my own, and I'm used to the mountains."

"I'm back in Boulder." He said it casually, hoping he saw interest on Bleu's face.

"Oh, wow. So you went back where it all started. Is it still wonderful?"

"It is. The hiking is still magical." He looked Bleu over. "Your shirt is all inside out."

Bleu pinked but rolled his eyes, then stripped the shirt off, leaving him bare-chested. Jesus. So damn pretty.

Ryan's fingers curled against his palms. "If it wasn't a graphic sweatshirt, it would be fine. Exposed seams are very in."

"Yeah, I'm blowing the 'prove that you're not a worthless asshole' thing, though."

"What?" Ryan blinked, taken aback. "You're amazing. You skied like an advanced beginner without even trying."

"Now I need to focus on dressing myself." Bleu laughed, but there was some embarrassment in it.

"You got it. Just shoes." He chuckled. "Does Floyd tell you if you're not wearing shoes?"

"No. Floyd cares not for my footwear." Bleu sighed. "It's weird, not having him here. Quartz is spoiling him for me."

"A puppy spa day?"

"Yes. God, Floyd loves to be brushed and have homemade Geoff treats."

It sounded pretty damn fine, honestly. He liked Geoff's treats.

"Hopefully he'll have pie or something tonight."

"Carb fiend," Bleu teased.

"I'm not on the circuit anymore. I can eat."

"Yeah?" Bleu reached out, stroking his belly. "You feel right."

"I work out like a monster because I'm vain." He chuckled, his belly bouncing against Bleu's hand.

"Do I look like you remember?"

God, that was a discussion to be had naked in bed.

He studied Bleu, though, giving the question the consideration it deserved. "Well, from what I've seen, you're you only… older, leaner, more defined. Like, you've grown into your face."

"Is that good?"

"Yes." He put all his admiration into the word. "Shoes. I'm starving."

"Right. Sorry." Bleu put on his shoes, tugged his jacket on.

"Is it Dan?" He needed to know who'd made Bleu so self-conscious. He hoped to hell it wasn't him, because that was a long while ago. Bleu had never been one to dwell.

"Is what Dan?"

"The way you're worried about being a burden."

"That's why we broke up, you know. Dan and I… our breakup wasn't a big deal. It was just an acknowledgment that I'm a giant redneck and he's a high-dollar suit from Santa Fe."

"But that doesn't mean you're pointless, you know." He'd never thought that, and he would feel like a massive ass if Bleu thought he did.

"I just don't want anyone to feel like they have to take care of me."

"Well, I want to take you to lunch." He gave Bleu a spontaneous hug. "You did so good."

Bleu didn't so much as stiffen; he grabbed hold and held on tight.

Oh. Bleu was starved for touch. Ryan held on as long as he could, but he let go when a gaggle of teenage boys came in. He let one hand linger on Bleu's arm. "Come on, babe."

"Yeah. I'm starving. So, tell me about Boulder. Do you have a house?"

"I have a condo right now that I'm renting. I wanted to find the right house, so I have a little over six months to hunt."

"Oh neat. So you get where I'm coming from."

"I do." He led Bleu, with shoes, out the door and to his SUV. The restaurant wasn't far, but it wasn't like walking was easy right now. The snow was beginning to fall again, making the world look like a fantasy land.

"I feel the snow." Bleu's joy was palpable, and he stuck out his tongue to catch snowflakes.

Ryan laughed, delighted. "What does it feel like, babe?"

"Tiny kisses."

"Mmm. Cold kisses." He chuckled some more, opening the car door for Bleu.

"Uh-huh. But they're sweet enough, right?"

"Right." He wanted to kiss that mouth, but he didn't dare. Bleu wasn't with him on that yet.

"So are we going far?"

"Nothing's far in Aspen."

Bleu snorted. "No, I guess not. It's just hard for me to tell."

"It's literally within walking distance of the lower lot, but I have a VIP spot."

"Ooh la la." Bleu laughed for him, leaned into him for a second. "What are you driving?"

Curious man.

"A GMC Terrain. I like how it drives like a car but off-roads like the sports utility it is." He had a mom car.

"Oh. Cool." Like Bleu knew. "Is it tall or short?"

"Uh. Middle, I guess. You don't have to hoist up in, but it's not low-slung."

"Good deal. I like knowing whether to bend or leap or slide."

"Lift and slide." He waited to make sure Bleu got in.

"Oh, leather. Sexy."

"Seat warmers too. Tell me if your butt gets too hot." He loved his seat warmers, but Phil had hated them, saying they made him sweat.

"Ooh. I love seat warmers!" Bleu bounced and clapped, just joyous as anything.

He laughed, so happy it hurt, and got them hamburger bound. "You going to get a yard where you can play in the snow in Santa Fe?"

"I need a yard for Floyd, yeah? But I need to be close to things too, you know, and I need studio space. It's all complicated."

"Oh, I bet in Santa Fe studios are easy."

"Mmm. A lot of them are in lofts in casitas or garages, though. Not ideal." Bleu shrugged. "And the good houses need cars. I'm not exactly car friendly."

"Mmm. Well, you'll figure it." He almost said *we'll*, which was cart well before horse.

"I will. I'm a smart dog." Bleu explored the seat, the dashboard, fingers moving over everything.

"You so are. Well, maybe Floyd is," Ryan teased. He parked only minutes later at CP Burger. "Ta-da. Can you smell burgers?"

"Onions. Mushrooms. Burgers. Bacon. Fries."

"Yeah." He breathed deep. Beef. That was about it. He loved that about Bleu. The man lived in a slightly different world, one where all his senses besides sight were bigger, deeper. He wondered what sorts of things Bleu's brain imagined.

He couldn't even fathom not knowing what colors were. Ryan shook his head. Hell, for all he knew, Bleu saw weird not-colors in his head. He certainly had no trouble with shapes.

"Are we okay?" Bleu was turned toward him, expression curious. "Do we need to wait for something?"

"Nope. I was just staring at you." He might as well admit it. "Watch your step. The lot is slushy."

"Are you coming around?"

"I am." He hopped out and damn near went ass over teakettle himself. "Whoa. Be right there."

"Be careful. Lord, I'm sore in the thighs." Bleu sat still, waiting for him.

"I hear you. All that cross-country I've been doing has my ass sore." He helped Bleu out of the car to move them inside. It was so much colder in street clothes.

"Yeah? Is it different than what we did today?"

"Oh, yeah. It's a whole different motion. Kinda like an elliptical. Have you done that?"

"I have. I've been in a gym a few times. I don't love it, though. They're loud and confusing."

"Well, cross-country is way less noisy. It's astounding how amazing it is out there once you get away from all the trappings of people. We should go."

"Okay." Just as easy as that. Okay.

The warmth in the restaurant made him shiver. Lord. It was really crunchy out there.

Bleu rubbed his arm, up and down, to warm him. "Poor frozen man."

"I know! It's ridiculous. I've spent more time in boardrooms and studios than I have outside lately."

"That doesn't sound like you."

"I know." He would have to chew that one over. "I think I just realized it."

"I need my time in the studio, but I love being outside. That's why—"

They were greeted at the counter, and he waved at a table. The lady working nodded once she realized Bleu couldn't see.

"Why what?" Ryan asked when they were seated.

"Huh?" Bleu pinked and grinned.

"That's why what? You got cut off." No hiding.

"That's why Dan and I broke it off. He worries about everything—me going out, me breaking things, starting a fire, everything."

"I can see that." He thought about Phil, and how everything was business over pleasure with that guy.

"Yeah. I know that I'm a challenge, but I do okay."

"I think you do great. Stuff gets broken. God knows I've broken skis and poles, bones, my mom's candy dish."

"I think I do great too. I wish I could drive. I think that would be the coolest."

"Yeah? I can probably make that happen." He had a buddy who was a race driver who volunteered for an organization similar to his. "Nothing at speed, but it can be done."

"Really? Seriously? You think so?" Ryan loved the light that shone from Bleu's face.

"I do. Justin would totally do it. It's all about coordinating a time."

"That would rock. I want to try. Just once." Bleu's fingers moved over the menu. "Is there a bacon cheeseburger?"

"There's a build your own, or a bacon and bleu. They have falafel, chicken or tuna too, and hot dogs."

"I'll do the bacon and bleu and onion rings, then. Bacon and bleu for Bleu."

"Will tots do it? They have parmesan fries too, just no rings." If Bleu wanted onion rings, they'd find a place.

"Tots work just fine. They'll go with the burger."

"Cool." He wanted the parm truffle fries and the "Fire" burger. "The bacon and bleu does have caramelized onions." He so rarely read the whole menu, but with Bleu, he needed to.

"I can handle that. Have you had Geoff's caramel onion and sausage flatbread? Oh my God."

"No. He's holding out on me. I'll ask for lunch maybe. I mean, not that he won't be busy the next few days."

"Yeah, he's catering the big party. I'm going to have to remember to leave them alone."

"Well, I bet they would still feed us." He hated the idea that Bleu didn't want to eat in the main dining room and might just hide in his cabin.

"Yeah. I mean, they'll bring me a meal too. Dan gets nervous eating in public with me."

"We'll see what Geoff and Stoney say." Quartz liked to have company when both his dads were working. "We could eat together, if they're busy. Hell, we could eat together regardless."

Bleu smiled, ducking his head again. "I might not need it, if these burgers taste as good as they smell."

They ordered from the very kind counter lady when she came over, and he got them a kale salad to start too. He really was grindy hungry. Bleu might surprise himself. Skiing was more exercise than you'd think.

It didn't take long for their food to come, and they tucked into it like starving people.

He had to admit that he didn't see where Bleu's ex got his worry. Bleu ate cleanly, easily, obviously unselfconscious. Never once had he been ashamed or worried to eat with Bleu.

"What are you thinking about so hard?" Bleu asked him.

"Huh? Watching you eat. I love how you love your food." Phil had been constant in his vigilance. Too many carbs, Ryan. Too much food. Got to watch your competition weight.

"Food is love, huh? You want a tater tot?"

"I do. Want a truffle fry?"

"Uh-huh." Bleu reached out and cupped Ryan's jaw, then fed him the bite with his other hand.

He hummed, then pressed a fry to Bleu's lips in return. It was intensely sexual, so intimate. And it was a goddamn french fry. He closed his eyes, feeling Bleu's lips move against his fingers.

Bleu's tongue touched his fingers, tasting him so gently.

He caught his breath, then laughed. "Tease."

"Sorry." Bleu didn't look particularly apologetic.

"Uh-huh. I just bet you are."

"What? I am. I totally am." Bleu ate another tot, a goofy smile on his face.

"You're something." *Something wonderful.*

"I'm a bunch of somethings. I'm special."

"You are." He licked his lips, the fire sauce making them tingle.

Bleu snorted for him, then nibbled on a bit of bacon from his burger. "Oh, this is good."

"Uh-huh. Damn good." He grabbed another fry, his eyes on Bleu's face. He could watch this for days. For weeks. Forever.

He skidded to a thought-stop right there. He was always getting ahead of himself. Bleu needed to get to know him again. He needed to get to know Bleu. He wanted to learn how Bleu reacted to being touched, whether he still loved superhot showers and a ton of pillows bunched up on the bed.

Ryan sure hoped so.

Bleu leaned back in his chair, sighing. "God, that was the ticket."

"Yeah. I was hungrier than I thought." He wiped a bit of mayo off Bleu's face.

"Thank you." Bleu grinned. "That was a juicy one."

"It was. I had goo on my arm even. You did way better." He didn't see any reason not to heap praise on something that was obviously a sore spot.

"Practice. Years of practice, baybee."

"Yeah, yeah." He stretched, feeling his back pop and crack. Lord, it was hell to get old. "You want anything else?"

Bleu's eyes opened comically wide. "There's no room for anything else, man."

"No, but we'll have to come back. They have adult milkshakes." Never let it be said that he didn't know how to tempt Bleu. They'd had that going on for a long time.

"Ice cream and booze? What's not to like?"

"Right?" He chuckled, patting his belly loud enough for Bleu to hear. "Not today, though."

"God no. You'll have to bring me back."

Score. Ryan didn't cheer, but he sure wanted to. "I can do that."

"Cool." Bleu grinned at him, eye lines crinkling at the corners.

"Yeah." They sat until they finished their drinks. "You ready, babe? It's just gonna get more and more crowded."

"Let's go back. I want to play with your heated seats."

"You got it." *Oh, good man.*

"Cool." Bleu grabbed his wallet from his pocket. "How much is the check?"

"I got this one, babe. You can get the next one, huh?"

"Are you sure? Thank you. I totally will."

"I am." He reached over to squeeze Bleu's hand. "It's been a great day so far."

"Yeah. Thanks for letting me stay."

"I'm glad you did. Heated seats, ahoy!" He was looking forward to the drive up to the ranch—him and Bleu, together in the car. For a good while.

Hell, maybe they'd sing.

Chapter Nine

BLEU hadn't had so much fun in ages—they sang all the way up the mountain, with Ryan telling him about the terrain, the snow, in between songs.

Ryan even saw a big buck elk on the side of the road, and Bleu made bugling noises for a while.

"Okay, where did you learn to do that?" Ryan asked.

"YouTube video." He'd loved the sound, just loved how it was like a brass hound dog noise.

"No shit? I didn't know you could learn that from YouTube."

"You can learn a shit-ton from the internet. More if you can see, I bet. You'd be surprised how many sites aren't accessible."

"Yeah. It's amazing how many movies aren't closed-captioned. Mom is having a harder time hearing, you know? All those years of machines."

"Yeah." Ryan's mom worked with those huge sewing machines, one of those places that were so dangerous, they wouldn't even let him visit. "Is it real bad or just irritating?"

"Mostly irritating. She has hearing aids, but she doesn't like them."

"Ah." He sort of felt sick, just at the thought. He didn't know how not to be blind, but deaf? Christ.

"Yeah. She's okay, but she would love to watch all her movies with closed-captioning."

"That's words on the screen, right?"

"Yep. They say what the people on the show do. Well, they're supposed to. Sometimes they just suck at typing."

"As bad as I do?"

They both laughed at that, because as well as Bleu managed, in college he'd been… miserable. Miserable and utterly illegible.

"Some of them, yeah. Maybe they have blind guys doing it!" Ryan was teasing him like mad.

"Oh, I bet I would love that job. I would fuck with people constantly." He'd make it seven seconds before he got fired.

Ryan hooted, laughing so hard, Bleu was worried about Ryan driving. Kinda. Okay, Ryan was an amazing driver. At least that's how it felt—no sudden stops and starts, it didn't feel squirrely on the road, and he didn't hear any stress in Ryan's voice.

Sometimes Dan was a little worried about snowy roads, which was silly. God knew they got snow in Santa Fe.

He chuckled. Dan came from a flat stretch of the Navajo reservation. Maybe it was curvy mountain roads that made him nervous.

"What are you laughing at, you?"

"I was thinking about how you're obviously comfortable driving in this weather."

"Oh, I love it. Shit, compared to driving in Chamonix or Turin, this is a breeze."

"Yeah?" He didn't know how to parse that, but he knew that navigating some places was easier than others.

"Both in the Alps, both with many more old European roads. They don't have guardrails so much. It can be hairy."

"Wow. Wow, that's cool. I went down into a kiva in Jemez that was like that." He hadn't known what to do, how to get back up and out. The ladders had been terrifying.

"Yeah? That's freaky for sure. I did the kiva at the Cliff Palace at Mesa Verde when I was a kid. My dad had to carry me out. Bad moment."

"Oh man. Really? This was hard. I made it, but I damn near killed myself."

"I just had a kiddie panic attack. It was full of people and yet dark." Ryan laughed, the sound low and wry. "I think the one at Jemez is way scarier now. Those rungs are huge and far apart."

"You've been there?" How cool was that? Jemez wasn't common knowledge, outside of New Mexico.

"Yeah, I was in Los Alamos for an airbrush guy. He does great work. He suggested Bandelier and Jemez."

"What were you getting airbrushed?"

"A snowboard. He was doing a painting for one that I was going to get sealed then."

"Sealed?" He wanted to know everything.

"Yeah. If you use a paint option like airbrush, you have to get serious sealant. Lacquer. But it still has to be a snowboard."

"So this is one for you to ride? Do you ride a snowboard?"

"One does. I shred on it." Ryan was teasing again.

"Shred. Is it fun?" Could he try it?

"It's amazing. It's so different from skiing."

"How? What's different? Do you have one I can touch? A snowboard?"

"I do. I have a couple in my cabin. And it's a different motion, a different speed, everything."

Finally Bleu asked what he wanted to ask. "Can I try?"

"Hell, yes." Ryan reached over to squeeze his hand. "I know a place where we can go for that where we'll have a great time."

He held on, his heart hiccupping a little bit. Oh damn. Damn. Ryan made him all fluttery.

"Thanks, baby," he murmured. "I would love to try."

"So we will. We can try anything."

"That's a pretty broad palette. Anything." He could think of a few anythings that involved him and Ryan and beds and lube….

"I'm willing." Ryan's voice lowered a whole octave.

"Me too." He drew a circle on Ryan's palm.

"Now you're gonna make me worry about driving, babe." Ryan's warm chuckle slid up his spine, but Ryan pulled away. They turned off on the ranch road. He could feel when it happened.

"Now we go straight up." He remembered.

"Yeah, and the SUV tells me it hates me." The engine began to whine, and Ryan's arm moved, downshifting, he bet.

"Is it okay?" He wasn't worried now, because they were here. Stoney would bring horses down for them, if he had to. He knew how to ride.

"Yeah, it's fine, babe. I would put on chains if I needed to. In fact, it's better than it was the other day coming up."

"Good deal." He knew that heavy snow could be way easier to walk on than a light sprinkling, so driving had to be the same.

"The sleighs are fun, though. Has Stoney ever given you a ride?"

"No, this is the first winter I've come up. I've been in the spring and summer."

"Oh man, okay. Well, when he hauls them out for the gala, we'll go."

"Yeah? That would be neat. I can sing 'Jingle Bells.'"

"You sing better than I do."

All of a sudden they flattened out, and soon after Ryan changed gears again. They coasted to a stop, and Bleu tried not to feel disappointed.

"That was a great drive. Seriously."

"It was." Ryan leaned close, kissing his cheek gently. "Thank you."

That kiss burned like a tiny ember had touched him.

They climbed out of the car, Bleu waiting for Ryan to come get him. He needed help in snow this deep. Ryan put his hand on one arm, and he held on as they headed out.

He heard Floyd pattering to him, the snow icy on top. "Floyd is coming!" Quartz yelled.

"I hear him! Hey, boy! Did you have a great day?" He reached down, and Floyd pushed right into his hand. That nose was cold! He groped a little and found Quartz hadn't put on Floyd's harness. Okay, he had

Ryan. He rubbed those cold ears with his other hand. "Hey, boy."

"Ryan!" That was a voice he didn't know, but the feet it belonged to moved almost as fast as Floyd's. He heard the sound of lips smacking on skin. "There you are. I put my stuff in the cabin, huh? Hot tub! God, honey. I never thought I'd get here. Is this your new student? Pleased to meet you. I hope you had fun on the slopes. Isn't he great? I ordered dinner for us, along with a bottle of champagne."

Bleu let go of Ryan's arm, his fingers searching for Floyd's harness, which of course wasn't there. Right.

"Bleu—" Ryan touched his shoulder, but he stepped back.

"Quartz? Could you give me a hand?"

"Do you need help, man? Ry and I can make sure you get somewhere safe before we start our night."

"No, thank you. I'm fine. Y'all have a good one." Please, he prayed. He just wanted to get to the cabin and get in the shower and… yeah. Just move. Just go.

"*Y'all*? Oh my God. How cute is that? A blind skiing Texan!"

"That's me. Cute as all fucking get-out. Quartz? You ready?"

"Yessir." Quartz put Bleu's hand on his arm. "This way."

"Bleu, wait!"

He ignored Ryan's shout. No, he wasn't doing this.

"Thanks, man," he told Quartz. "Uh. I don't suppose you noticed if my friend Dan was here?"

"No, sir. He called and left a message for you that he was spending a couple days in Aspen."

"Excellent. Thank you. What do I owe you for your work today?" He hoped he didn't look as hurt as he was. As ashamed. God, he was an idiot. Of course Ryan wasn't single. He hadn't even bothered to ask.

"Nothing. Floyd and I had so much fun. Did you have fun?"

"I did. I skied. I would try it again." Some day.

"Do you want me to bring you some supper?"

"No, thank you. I'm going to take a shower and a long nap." He was beginning to shiver a little bit.

The blind Texan. How *cute*.

"Okay. Are you all right?" Quartz sounded a little worried.

"I don't feel so well." He didn't lie, because people knew. "I got too hot in the car."

"Oh. I do that and it makes me throw up. You're here. I'm sorry I forgot to harness Floyd."

"No. No, he was off work. You did just right. Are you sure I don't owe you anything?" He had cash in his wallet, and if Quartz said no again, he'd give it to Stoney to hand over.

"Yep. I love Floyd! He's way easier to bathe than a basset hound. Call us if you need us." Quartz let him and Floyd into the cabin before running off.

"Will do." He closed the door and grabbed his cane, which was right by the entry. "Cute blind Texan. Christ. Christ, Ryan, you should've said."

Someone should have said.

He stripped down and went to get in the tub and soak. He was sore, down near his bones. Down deep.

RYAN turned on Phil, pushing his ex's chest. "What was that about?"

"Huh? I just haven't seen you in a while, Ry. I wanted to celebrate, have a little fun. You know?" Phil was wide-eyed, pretty green gaze searching his.

He sighed. "Sorry. Sorry I snarled. You just—I mean, I didn't expect this at all."

Phil took his arm. "Come on. We'll bubble and warm up. I'm freezing my nuts off. You look great, by the way. Happy."

"Thanks. Thanks." He let Phil lead him to the cabin, but Ryan pulled away when they got inside. "I can't do this now, Phil."

"Okay… did I do something wrong?"

"No. Oh, hon, I'm sorry." He sat on his bed. "I just—the Texan? He and I were a thing in college. He's even more amazing now."

"The blind guy? No shit? Are you two… you know…."

"Well, I was going to try to seduce him tonight. Until last night I thought he was married." Ryan shook his head, feeling like a giant asshole.

"No shit?" Phil chuckled and rolled his eyes. "And then I come up with the whole hot tub thing. Go team me. Shit, man, I'm sorry."

"Yeah." He chuckled. "He's rooming with his ex too. I guess they wouldn't let me in." He would talk to Bleu tomorrow. Alone.

"Ouch. Well, is his ex hot? When you two hook up, maybe I can get laid too." Christ, Phil was a shit. Charming as anything, but a bit of a horndog.

"He's a burly, and yes, pretty, Native American. He's very… precise."

"Sounds lovely. So… no hot tub? I can put my shorts on."

"No hot tub for me. But I'll have supper and champagne." He wasn't going for drunk, but relaxed would be better.

"Fair enough." Phil reached out and patted his thigh. "I'm sorry I fucked up your hookup."

"Me too, but it's good to see you." It was, really. He liked Phil even if he didn't love the guy.

"Yeah, you too." Phil leaned back. "Even if I thought I had a guaranteed friends-with-benefits situation with you."

"Shut up."

They both laughed.

"Seriously," Ryan said. "There will be no shortage of gay skiers for the next couple of days."

"Yeah. Yeah, you'll have to point out the lusty ones."

"There's a cook who works here. He can totally point out the horny dudes."

"Fair enough. So, tell me everything about Mr. Cutie Patootie. I want to know who's worth giving up all this."

Lord. He hoped dinner came before he killed Phil. That didn't stop him from telling the man about everything, though, did it?

No, sir. He could fucking rhapsodize about Bleu Bridey for days on end.

Chapter Ten

BLEU'S phone rang, and he fumbled for it. "Who is it?"

The phone's tinned voice answered, "Stoney River."

"Answer." He sat up and stretched. "Hey, man."

"Hey, Bleu. I want to bring you supper. Is it okay if I come on?"

"Sure. Sure, I… what time is it?"

"A little after nine. I know it's late. I was worried when you didn't call or come to the kitchen, but I just got off duty at the great room."

"Oh, you're… that's damn kind, Stoney. Thank you." He got up and started throwing clothes on.

"No problem. I'll be down in about ten."

"Thanks."

They hung up, and that gave him time to get dressed and feed Floyd, which he felt total guilt about, and let Floyd out too.

Lord, it was cold out there, crisp enough that he couldn't quite breathe. He rubbed his arms, straining to hear… what? Laughter? Raised voices. There was plenty of both, but none of it was Ryan.

No. Ryan was hot tubbing and champagning and having wild monkey sex. That was an indoor sport in this weather.

Floyd shook right next to him before trotting inside. "Everyone is an asshole today."

"Hopefully not me," Stoney said, making Bleu jump.

"No. Not you and not your son, who is an amazing kid, and I appreciate him so much."

"He had the best time. He's great with dogs, and ours are all ranch mutts who don't want spa days." Stoney stepped inside past him. "Chilly out there."

"It is."

"You mind if I turn on the lights, man?"

He chuckled. "Y'all have lights in here?"

"We do! Vampires like you and Floyd may not need them, but I do." Something smelled really good.

"Lasagna?"

"Good nose. There's salad and garlic toast too."

"Thanks, Stoney. I know y'all are crazy busy."

"Yeah, I'd say it's the season, but we're just busy. Not that I'm complaining. It's a blessing and I know it."

"It is."

Stoney shifted from foot to foot, the floor creaking. "You okay, Bleu? Quartz said you looked pained."

"I—" Shit. "I sorta made a fool of myself, buddy. Over Ryan Shields. Exes, you know."

"Oh, ouch." Stoney went silent a second. "Was he mean? I know y'all had a fight last night."

"No. He was my ski instructor, believe it or not, and it was so fucking fun, man." So damn fun, and Ryan had been…. Oh, what the fuck did it matter? He didn't cheat, and he didn't sleep with cheaters.

"Oh." Stoney just sighed. "Well, that's good, right?"

"It was. It was a killer day, but I—I didn't know he was involved. Totally my fault, I didn't ask, but…." But he hadn't known, and he had been thinking pornalicious thinks about Ryan.

"Oh. Oh! Phil showed up, didn't he?"

"Yeah." And so everyone knew. God. "Anyway. I'm cool. Just a little embarrassed. I didn't do anything I'd be ashamed of."

"No, of course not." Stoney paused, then took a breath. "Are you sure they're still a thing? Phil has always seemed kinda… indifferent."

"They were fixin' to hot tub with champagne." That hadn't sounded indifferent at all.

"Oh."

"Yeah."

"I'm sorry if I butted in. Quartz said Dan wasn't coming back tonight. Did you want to come to the house?"

"Aren't y'all busy?" He shook his head. "Let's share supper, man. I'd like to visit."

"Sure." Stoney chuckled. "It's quiet down here."

"Isn't it? I could hear some bustle up toward the house, but here the snow hides a lot."

"It does. It muffles things." Stoney sat down across from him, beginning to unwrap supper.

"So are you having a good ski week? Do you like this?" He couldn't imagine all the moving parts of running a place like this—keeping all the balls in the air.

Stoney laughed softly. "You know what? It's insane, but I love it. I'm home with my husband and my boy and my best friends. I have my horses and my mountains and enough to keep me busy and let me sleep hard at night. That's all a cowboy can ask for in life."

Bleu blinked hard at that. God, Stoney meant it. There was no manufacturing that joy.

"How about you? You liking it here?"

"Oh, I am. I like the company. I'm going to have to get back to work soon, though. Be useful as well as ornamental."

"Well, I sure appreciate the way you are with Quartz. He's had the best time. Snow horrors. Dog sitting."

"He's a good kid. I like him." Stoney had done a great job raising him.

"Thanks. How do you want me to set up your plate?"

"Just tell me where it is when you give it to me."

"You got it. So what do you do at home?"

"For food?" He chuckled. "I eat a lot of sandwiches, honestly. And a lot of pizza, but that's just because it's easier."

"If I get too nosy just say so, hon." Stoney chuckled. "Quartz gets it from me. Wanting to know everything."

"I don't mind. You know that I'm living alone again. It's the weirdest thing, the first couple of nights alone in a new place."

"I bet."

Stoney probably never had lived alone. From home to college to the ranch….

He hadn't done it much, but he'd done it and he didn't suck at it, not entirely. Bleu chuckled. "It's especially weird when you can hear things but not see them. Floyd is awesome, though."

"He is so smart. I've never met one that was so clever. He was doing tricks with Quartz."

"Was he?" He clapped his hands. "Oh, I wish I could see."

"Here, let me see if he remembers. Speak, Floyd. Speak."

A low woof made him laugh out loud. "Good boy!"

"Spin, Floyd."

The dog's claws tapped as he moved, the sound familiar, weirdly musical.

"Okay, now call him to you."

"Floyd. Come here, boy."

"Now hold out your hand and say high five."

He grinned, feeling a touch silly, but put his hand out. "High five!"

Floyd's paw hit his hand, firm and sure.

"Dude! How cool is that? I didn't know you knew tricks." He knew that Floyd was his lifeline and his best friend, but silly dog tricks hadn't been in their training.

"Quartz was ecstatic." Stoney pushed him a plate. "So the lasagna is at the bottom, like closest to you. Is that six?"

"Yep. Perfect. You said bread and salad too?"

"Yeah. Bread is at twelve, while salad is in a little bowl to the right of your plate. Your right. Geoff didn't want it to get hot."

"I love the smell of italian dressing."

He heard Stoney sniffing. "Huh. It does smell, don't it? How cool is that?"

"And red wine vinaigrette smells different from zesty italian." Scents were amazing.

"I like ranch best, but Geoff makes this weird salad where he soaks tomatoes in red wine vinaigrette that rocks."

"Layer salad? My momma makes that."

"Yeah? The one with green olives and bacon?"

"Yes! I'll have to ask Geoff where he found it." That was funny. Oh, he missed that stuff sometimes. He needed to call Momma. He'd been there for Christmas, introducing the family to Floyd, enjoying Austin.

"Mmm. That's good." Stoney was not a noisy chewer. That was nice.

The lasagna was cheesy and spicy and just wonderful. He did love a casserole. The salad had a nice bite, with romaine and cherry tomatoes and homemade croutons. Bless Geoff's heart.

"This is amazing."

"Uh-huh. Try the garlic bread. It's the best."

He found the hefty chunk of baguette, the mixture of crisp and buttery like magic. The garlic was just enough to make his tongue tingle. Geoff really was a treasure.

"Yum." Bleu laughed. "Thank you so much for coming down. I was feeling low."

"You know it. I'm sorry your evening got fucked-up, huh?"

"Yeah, me too, but it is what it is, right?" Ryan hadn't made him any promises, after all. His expectations were his issue.

"It is. Still makes a man crazy." They ate the rest of their meal, the talk changing to small things—snow and horses, green chile and salsa. The little important things.

"Well, I need to go tell Quartz good night." Stoney's chair scraped back.

"Thanks for the company, sir. I know it's taking you from your family." He couldn't express how much he appreciated the care.

"Oh, they made me go. They said I needed a quiet supper with a friend." Stoney touched his shoulder. "Thank you."

"Thanks, man. Seriously. Oh, I need to give you a twenty for your son. He wouldn't take any money from me."

"Neither will I," Stoney said. "If you'd have seen him, you would know he had the best time, and he got out of chores."

"Are you sure? I don't mind at all."

"I know, hon. I really appreciate the thought, but the ranch will pay him too. It will go into his college fund."

"All right. If you're positive." He didn't want to offend, that was for sure.

"I am. You're a good guy." Stoney shuffled a little. "Do you need anything else?"

"Nope. Go." He grinned, waved his hands. "Shoo."

"Night, Bleu." Stoney left him, the door closing with a click.

"It's good to have friends, right, Floyd?" He heard Floyd's tail brushing on the floor. "I saved you a bite, huh?"

Bleu fed a morsel to Floyd, careful because that was a lot of nightshade.

He sighed softly and turned on his tablet. Music filled the air, and he leaned back, letting the sound pour over him. The rest was just water under the bridge.

RYAN woke up the next morning feeling sore and grumpy.

He glanced over at Phil's bed, but the man was gone. Probably off to see if Dan was at breakfast. The idea of a rich, hot Santa Fean really revved his engine.

Not that Ryan could even be pissed. Phil had been decent, had listened to him until the wee hours, had kept all his clothes on.

Too bad he wasn't Bleu.

Rising, Ryan decided to grab a shower and then head up to the kitchen to beg a not-public meal. If he was lucky, there would be a certain Texan doing the same.

He just needed the chance to explain.

A hot shower had him in a better mood in moments. He dressed for warmth, because his smartwatch said it was just fifteen out there.

At least two feet of snow had fallen overnight, and the cowboys had been out shoveling, obviously. There were paths carved out and little ski poles marking the path, their rainbow ribbons waving in the breeze.

He stomped the snow off his boots before climbing the steps, which had those heated ice melters on them. That was an excellent idea. Tapping lightly before he entered was the polite thing to do, but Geoff met him with a smile.

"Hey, Ryan! Come on in!"

"Thanks. Woo, it's chilly."

"You know it. Oatmeal? I have that and cinnamon rolls."

"Oatmeal, I think. I'll take a cinnamon roll for the road." The kitchen table always looked so inviting, scarred and golden with age. Ryan sat, leaning back a little when Geoff put coffee in front of him. "Have you, uh, seen Bleu?"

"Not yet. He hasn't peeked in. He will. He'll need coffee."

"If he doesn't show soon, I'll go get him. That path is icy."

"Good deal." A cup of coffee and a bowl of oats appeared in front of him. "Milk and goodies are on the table."

"Thank you." He beamed at Geoff, though the poor guy looked a little harried.

"What can I do? You look stressed."

"Tiny threw his back out shoveling last night. I'm gonna be in the weeds if he doesn't get up and about."

"Well, I'm no chef, but I can chop and carve meat."

"You are a guest, Ryan."

"So? I'm not doing anything right now. I can deliver room service if you need. I have great snow legs."

"Oh, you're a love. I swear to make you anything you want for lunch."

Oh. Oh, what had Bleu said he'd loved so much? "Sausage and onion flatbread?"

Geoff cackled like a raven. "Bleu's favorite."

"Make that and I will do anything you need." There. Now he could make Bleu come to lunch with him so he could tell the man all about Phil.

"Fair enough. Eat your breakfast, and I'll get your help."

Ford came bustling in, arms full of empty platters. "Here for a refill, man."

"What do you need?"

"Toast and bacon."

"You got it."

Ryan ate his breakfast fast, genuinely wanting to help Geoff, who was slinging bacon onto trays. He jumped up as soon as he was done, grabbed bread to stuff in the line of toasters. "Do I butter?"

"Please. Thank you."

Ford chuckled. "Putting your ass to work, is he?"

"I volunteered." Ryan grinned. "I'm begging a special lunch, and he told me Tiny was out."

"Yeah. Too much preshoveling sex."

He hooted. "At least someone is having it."

Ford didn't say anything, but when Ryan glanced over at him, he turned bright red.

"Yeah, yeah," Geoff muttered. "Both of you shut up."

"Hey, I had exactly as much sex as you did last night, man."

"I bet my dry spell is the longest." Geoff threatened him with a spatula.

"Yeah, that might be so." His wasn't… prodigious.

"I plead the fifth," Ford murmured. "I'm going in. Can you bring toast, Ryan?"

"You bet." He buttered the first stack after putting in more bread.

It was comfortable, working with Geoff, side by side. He liked it. This was part of what he was trained to do, right? Outdoor recreation had a hospitality element to it.

Hell, he just wanted something to do until he could talk to Bleu.

When he got back from delivering toast and avoiding Phil, Geoff had a whole set of trays for him to deliver. The best part was the insulated pizza bag he could carry all the domed dishes in.

He hadn't had so much fun in a while, and he met a bunch of men he wouldn't have otherwise, and got three phone numbers on the way.

Not that he needed them.

"Hey, Bleu called in, and I have his oats and all," Geoff said. "You want to deliver?"

"God yes. You're a prince, Geoff."

"I added an extra cup of coffee and cinnamon roll. You're off duty. Quartz is on now."

"Thanks." He gave Geoff a hug, because Geoff was an exceptional hugger. Bleu couldn't say no if he was on delivery, right?

Right. Okay. Go see Bleu and explain.

He headed down to the cabin and tapped on the door. *Come on, Bleu. Open up.*

The door swung open, Bleu standing there in a pair of tiny sweats and a trashed Sesame Street T-shirt.

"Hey, babe. Geoff sent breakfast. They're shorthanded, so I helped." He held his breath, waiting to see what Bleu was up to.

"Oh. Thank you. Come in." Bleu stepped back to let him through the door. Floyd was curled up by the gas fireplace, and he got a single wag.

"Hey, Floyd." He set the bag on the table so he could unload. "Okay, I'm going to start before you politely send me on my way," Ryan said, lifting domes off plates. "Phil and I haven't been together for six months. He was hoping for a booty call."

"I—" Bleu's expression was pure shock. "You… you don't have to explain."

"Yes, I do, because I don't want you to run off after the party and never speak to me again. I knew he was coming, but we're only sharing a cabin because they're so full up. I actually thought about getting him a hotel in Aspen when Ford told me they'd put us together."

"Oh. That-that's really good to know. Really." Bleu reached out, fingers searching for him.

Ryan took Bleu's hand and drew him close. "I'm sorry I didn't come last night. Phil is… well, he's a force of nature, and it took me a while to explain everything."

"It's okay. You don't have to explain to me."

"Yes, I do. I wasn't leading you on yesterday. I want to spend time with you. I want to get to know you again. Phil misunderstood me not kicking his ass out. He wants to meet Dan."

"Dan? Dan's in Aspen with a booty call, I think. He isn't here."

"Oh, well, Phil is never really lonely." He chuckled, then hugged Bleu. "Hungry?"

"I am. Uh… have you eaten?"

Oh. Okay, that wasn't a "please leave." That was "can you stay?"

"Geoff sent me a cinnamon roll. Is it okay if I stay?"

"You can. I'll start the fire and warm it up in here." Bleu tapped along with his cane to the fireplace and turned it on easily.

"Thanks." He set breakfast up on the little two-seater table. "Oats and all the good accompaniments. Cinnamon roll. Fruit."

"Coffee?"

"Yep. This one is yours. Smells good too."

"Yum." Bleu joined him at the table easily. "Thanks."

Bleu explored the edges of the bowl, then found a spoon.

"Do you want nuts and cinnamon sugar? Blueberries?"

"Yeah. Everything."

"Even the cream?" he teased. He knew Bleu liked cream in his coffee and whipped, but not really in oats.

"No. No cream, please. That's not good."

"I know, babe. I had to make a little fun." He stirred in fixings before handing over the bowl. "Ta-da."

"Thank you." Bleu took a spoonful and ate a bite, humming softly. "Oh, that's nice."

"It is. I ate a bowl, and now I will have dessert." He took the dome off the bigger of the two pastries.

Bleu inhaled deep. "Cinnamon rolls."

"Uh-huh. I have one for you too." Geoff was such a romantic.

"Cool. I love that smell." Bleu licked his spoon. "It's warm and homey, but a little exotic too."

"The cinnamon makes my nose tingle."

"Yeah?" Bleu put the bowl down and picked up his coffee, then drank deep.

"Are we okay, babe?" He needed to hear it.

"I just… I made assumptions."

"What kind? Because I was giving strong signals. I just—Phil took me by surprise. We went out with a whimper because we were never serious, so for him to be all booty call ready was a shock." He wanted Bleu to know he was totally ready for assumptions.

"Yeah? If Dan asked me for one, I'd probably be shocked too. We stopped sleeping together long before we broke up."

Okay, that was unexpected. Endearingly honest.

"Phil and I could have sex, but we never talked about anything but business." Ryan answered honesty with the same.

"I could talk to you for hours about everything, whether or not we had sex."

No one had ever said anything more wonderful to him.

"Thank you. I feel the same way." He reached over to touch Bleu's hand, and Bleu met him, touching his palm with a careful caress.

All he could do was hum, wanting more but not willing to push too hard.

"Of course, I really want to have sex, Ry. Wild, passionate monkey sex."

"Me too." His heart started to race. "With you."

"Yeah. I remember it fondly."

"Fondly?"

"Warmly?" Bleu began to grin.

"Cordially?" he asked, laughing.

"Desperately." Now that sounded more like it.

"Now?" Hopeful. Ryan was going for hopeful.

"Do you mind that my bed isn't made or that I have coffee breath?"

"Not one bit." He didn't care about any of that. "I have cinnamon mouth. It'll be great."

"You should kiss me. What if it doesn't work between us?" Bleu couldn't tease worth a shit.

"Oh, right, maybe it's changed." Ryan leaned over the table to press his lips to Bleu's.

It took a second, like they were both in shock, then Bleu reached up and cupped his jaw. They tilted just so, and damn if they weren't all lit up, all of a sudden.

He scooted around the table, needing to get closer, needing to touch. Right now.

"Ryan?" Bleu sounded worried, and Ryan realized he'd pushed back Bleu's chair and everything was a little precarious.

"Sorry. Sorry, but only if I scared you. Not for the kisses. Come sit on the bed with me."

"Uh-huh. Bed. God, you taste good."

He rose, then tugged Bleu up before sorta dancing them to the bed. Ryan loved to dance with Bleu, but there were things he liked more. Currently he was voting for nudity and lots of rubbing.

"This is the cutest shirt ever," Ryan said while he eased it off over Bleu's head.

"Is it? I love how soft it is." Bleu's nipples were tight, hard, begging for his touch.

He wasn't going to disappoint, either. Ryan pinched them both, a promise of sorts. That earned him a gasp and the prettiest little blush. The way Bleu twisted to get away, then get more, made him smile. "Pretty man."

Bleu reached for him, hands sliding up along his arms toward his face. He stilled, knowing Bleu wanted to see him before they moved on. Some things didn't change. Bleu's fingers moved over his face, finding his mouth, his nose, his eyes. The touches were sure, curious, and familiar.

He smiled wider, closing his eyes to let Bleu explore. God, he'd missed this.

"Beautiful. I could sculpt you for hours."

"Maybe later? Touch me now instead." Ryan kissed Bleu's fingers.

"Later." Bleu wrapped his hands around his scalp and drew him in for a kiss.

He kissed that sweet mouth, pressing inside with his tongue. He wanted to taste Bleu again, and Bleu was more than willing, opening right up for him with a low moan.

They kissed slow and long, learning angles, touching here and there. It was like making out with your high school sweetheart, except he didn't have to worry about his dad finding him.

Not at all. Maybe Phil and Dan.... He shook off that thought as a horror movie idea.

"What? What's wrong?" Sensitive little fucker.

"Oh, I had a vision of Dan and Phil bursting in." Might as well be honest. "It gave me a shudder."

"Lock the bedroom door. He's sleeping in the other room anyway." *Smart.*

Ryan got up to lock the door. "How did you get a two bedroom and I got stuck with my ex in a double queen?" He knew how. They'd thought he and Phil were still together.

"I'm special. Sparkly. Charming. All the good things."

"Uh-huh." He sat back down, sticking his cold hands against Bleu's ribs.

"Oh!" Bleu's eyes went wide and he arched, lips parted. He swooped in and took a hard kiss.

"Mmmph." He did love to laugh when he was making love.

Bleu was all over him, hands stripping his clothes away. He'd forgotten how good Bleu was at this, how easy the man was in his skin.

Ryan was hard and aching, his body ready for the main event even as his brain wanted him to take his time.

"I can smell you." Bleu climbed into his lap and rubbed them together.

"Well, I want you, so that's good, right?" He gripped Bleu's ass.

"Uhn." That worked as a yes. Bleu's belly pressed against his chest, the connection between them fiery.

God, this was still as good as it ever had been. Bleu had a few more ropey muscles now, a little more body fuzz. A couple of hot little scars that proved Bleu'd been living.

Ryan traced one with his fingers. "What happened?"

"I got hit by a motorcycle that ran a light."

"Oh God. Was it bad?" The scar itself had to have hurt, but broken bones and such were always worse.

"It wasn't fun, but I made it. It all happened very fast."

"I bet. I collided with another boarder once, and I came right out of my boots." He moved his fingers to Bleu's hip.

"Scary. You go fast." Bleu stroked his nipples before pinching lightly.

"I do." He'd been in the hospital for two weeks. He wasn't going to ruin the mood.

"We'll count scars after we fuck like rabid bunnies, fair?"

"Sounds like a plan, babe." He pushed Bleu down on his back.

Bleu stretched out for him, unashamed, lovely. Hard as a rock.

Ryan had to grab that thick cock and stroke it a few times. Bleu arched into his hand, driving up into his fingers like he needed nothing else in all the world.

"So pretty, babe. You're so damn pretty." Did that even mean anything to Bleu?

"God, I love how I look in your voice."

"Yeah? You're stunning to me." No one had ever been as amazing.

He leaned down and licked, his tongue dragging along Bleu's shaft, the flavor exploding over his tongue.

"Oh! Oh, hello." Bleu arched and twisted for him, one hand landing on his head. "Missed you."

He had a million words. Good thing he had his mouth full so he didn't spill them. Not yet.

Besides, Bleu could feel how Ryan needed. He knew.

He stroked, fascinated by the sight of Bleu's cock appearing and disappearing between his fingers. He lapped around the tip, traced the slit with the tip of his tongue.

Bleu cried out, the sound almost musical.

He nuzzled and licked, drawing more and more of those sounds from his Bleu. Ryan wanted all of them, didn't want to share them with anyone else down the line.

"Making me dizzy. Don't stop. God, Ry. Don't stop."

"Mmm." No way. He tugged the heavy balls, then stroked Bleu's thighs, spreading his lover wide. Bleu moved easily, trusting him. He wanted to lick and suck every part of that fine body. He nuzzled the white-blond curls, tugging them with his teeth.

"Ryan!" Bleu tried for scandalized, he thought, but didn't make it.

"Uh-huh?" he teased.

"Do it again."

"Okay." He tugged, pressing his chin against Bleu's balls.

Bleu arched up toward him with a happy little cry. So tactile and responsive. Those rough fingers tangled in his hair, stinging his scalp.

He groaned, climbing back up Bleu's body to steal another kiss, another bite.

Wrapping around him, Bleu made this joyful noise, licking at his lips. He'd forgotten this—the open, eager sounds, the way Bleu threw himself into their lovemaking.

They rocked together, cocks sliding one against the other—slick and hot. Bleu hooked one leg around him, dragging them alongside each other.

He moaned, needing more kisses. Ryan loved how Bleu tasted, loved every little uneven breath. Bleu rolled them, ending up straddling his waist, hands dragging down his chest.

"Bossy!" He laughed, stretching out long.

"Need to see. You get to see all the time."

"I'm right here for you to explore." *Anything, anytime.*

Bleu's expression went sharp then, and those hands began to map him. Face and neck, shoulders, chest—God, no one touched him like this.

"You're bigger, but not. Does that make sense?"

"I've put on more muscle. I had to. I'm not twenty anymore."

"No. Neither of us are. You're grown-up."

"So are you, babe. Sculptor's muscles." Ryan ran his hands up Bleu's arms.

Bleu measured his waist, then trailed up his six-pack.

He laughed. "I know, right? I need more body fat."

Bleu leaned down and licked his belly, the action shocking the hell out of him. He drew in a breath, his skin rising up with goose bumps.

"I remember this. I remember how you taste."

"Do you? God, that feels good, Bleu."

"I do. You're the best whiskey on earth." Bleu drew circles around his hips with callused thumbs.

"Am I?" Ryan chuckled. They were like whiskey, rough and pure fire.

"God yes." Bleu found his nipple, biting the tip, teasing him.

He arched his back, pressing into that heated touch. Bleu's mouth made him a little crazy. And Bleu's hands? Christ. Nothing compared to the way they molded him. They were magic.

The rounded slopes of Bleu's ass were perfect and firm, so he squeezed them. Bleu rippled, a low cry filling the air.

"You're needing," Ryan muttered.

"You have no idea."

"What do you want most, babe?" He would give this man anything.

"I want to fly with you. You always made me ache."

"I hear that." He rubbed the small of Bleu's back.

Bleu cupped his balls, rolling them slowly, easily, giving him just enough pressure. His toes curled, and Ryan grunted, drawing his belly in.

"Mmm." Bleu's grin was pure-D wicked.

"Uh-huh. You're something else, babe."

"I want you to fuck me. Hard."

"Oh hell yes." He hoped Bleu had condoms. Lube. The important things.

One way or the other, they would get the deed done.

He slid a finger along Bleu's crease. "Do you have the stuff?"

"Stuff? You mean lube and protection? I have lube in my bag and a rubber in my wallet like a good man."

"Oh ho! Smart." He kissed Bleu hard, letting himself drive in like he needed to.

Bleu moaned for him, bracing on his chest and kissing him right back. He had dreams like this. They ended badly. This was going to go well.

This was going to end with his cock buried to the root in Bleu, and both of them shooting hard.

"Where's your wallet, babe?"

"On the dresser by my phone."

Ryan lifted Bleu away from him so he could rise. "Don't run off."

"Where would I go? I want to be here."

The simple words made his heart swell bigger than the Grinch's at the end of the story.

Bleu leaned back against the headboard, hand sliding on his cock.

"Now don't get too far ahead," Ryan teased. It took forever to find a condom and the little tear-open pack of lube.

"I promise. I'm just waiting patiently."

"Or not so patiently." Ryan moved back to the bed, sitting beside Bleu's hip.

"This is patient!" God, he loved Bleu's laughter.

"I guess it is. You could have been whacking off like crazy."

"I could have. This is way more fun."

"Is it?" He opened the lube, getting his fingers wet, saving a little back for the deed itself.

"Mm-hmm. Way." Bleu was listening to him, head cocked.

"I like that." He stroked Bleu's cock, his hand closing over Bleu's. He used his other hand to press against that sweet hole.

Bleu's expression went slack, his lover moaning low.

"Uh-huh. Sweet." He slid a lubed finger inside.

God, Bleu was as tight as a virgin, body squeezing him like a vise. He shivered at how amazing that felt, licking his lips.

"I want more, Ry. Give me another."

"I got you, babe." He slipped another finger in, then added a tiny bit more lube. That was good stuff. Bleu let his head fall back, and Ryan watched him swallow convulsively. Bleu's chest rose and fell fast, a light flush working across his skin. "You make my mouth dry."

Bleu grinned, pushing back on Ryan's touch, riding him fearlessly. That tight, tiny hole closed around his fingers, the muscles working. God, he wanted in, but he wanted to make sure Bleu was good and ready for him.

"You're so slow." Bleu wiggled.

"You're impatient." He added a third finger and took a kiss in the same motion.

"Mmm." Bleu ran both hands down his back, tracing each bump of his spine. He pressed closer, almost like he was trying to join them on the cellular level.

Ryan pushed in and pulled out for as long as he could bear. Then he covered his cock with the condom so he could slick himself up.

Bleu reached out, fingers brushing the tip of Ryan's cock, nudging it firmly.

"I'm coming, babe. I swear." He muscled up between those spread legs.

"I've waited a long time, and I didn't even know it."

"I know. I know exactly how you feel." Ryan hummed, pushing into Bleu a scant inch.

Bleu's face went lax, a deep inhalation filling his lungs.

"That's it, babe. Breathe with me."

"You're… damn. Damn, you're real."

As real as they fucking came. He was going to make sure Bleu felt him, make sure every sense was filled to the brim. "I'm real, and I'm right here, Bleu."

"I want to see you." Bleu reached up, and Ryan bent into the touches. "Oh yes."

Bleu's smile was like the sun cresting the mountain after a perfect snow.

He rocked his hips down, letting Bleu feel him as he sank in, burying himself in that amazing heat. His eyes threatened to close, but he refused to let them. He wanted to see every second.

That face was unguarded, each expression right there for Ryan to see. Sweet and wanton, totally focused on what they were creating together—Christ, he burned to be half the man Bleu's face said he was.

He wanted to be now, more than he ever had.

They moved together, Ryan pressing deep, seating himself the whole way.

Bleu grabbed his ass and held on tight, keeping him deep and letting him feel the sweet muscles rippling.

His breath left him, his chest heaving. God, every squeeze and clench made his balls ache. Ryan gritted his teeth, holding on as hard as he could.

"Move. Move for me, please."

"Anything." Ryan moved, heavy thrusts that shook the bed. Bleu took him—every fucking inch, open and eager and begging for it. They were cooking with oil, sweat running on their skin. Bleu held nothing back, crying out with each thrust.

His asscheeks clenched, his belly pulling in. Nothing had ever been as good as Bleu. No one.

"Jesus…." Bleu started jacking himself, pulling hard and fast.

"Stay with me, babe. I want us to go together."

"Fuck yes. I want this to last and last."

Ryan nodded, straining hard, all his muscles engaged and working. "Great damn workout."

"Better than a gym, huh?"

"God yes. Better than anything."

Bleu cried out for him, and then he grabbed his knees and tugged, spreading himself until Ryan thought he might squeak.

Ryan gave him what he needed, slamming into Bleu hard. He watched every second, his cock spreading that tiny hole wide. They couldn't last much longer, so he kissed Bleu hard, wanting more contact.

Bleu's sigh was pure bliss, and he felt Bleu clench around him.

"Hot. Tight. Oh, babe." He was so close. So close.

"Soon. Please, Ry. Please."

"I'm right there. I just—"

Bleu squeezed him again, fierce enough he shouted, and that was the end of it. Ryan shot so hard his teeth rattled, and his Bleu followed right behind, sobbing with his need, seed spraying.

They collapsed together, panting, both as sweaty as if they'd been skiing for hours.

"Damn." Bleu kissed his temple. "That was… damn."

"And then some, babe. Thank you."

Bleu laughed softly, body squeezing him. "Can we do it again?"

"Yes. Just give me a moment to catch my breath and get another condom."

"Fair enough." That laugh filled the air, low and husky and well-fucked.

"Mmm. Good thing we have cinnamon rolls."

"Mm-hmm. I'll call for pizza and Cokes later. Much later."

"Flatbreads. Geoff promised."

"Oh, you do love me."

The words dropped between them, and Bleu turned bright red.

He just kissed that sweet mouth, not ready to make a mess of things just yet. "I got your back, babe."

"Thank you." Bleu closed his eyes, resting back against the pillows.

"Mmm." No, no hiding. He kissed Bleu's forehead, then his cheeks. Bleu lifted his chin, letting him explore.

He licked at a bead of sweat. "Say you'll spend the day with me, babe? One step at a time."

"I'd love to. I have a big bathtub. It's not a hot tub, but we can both fit."

"That sounds perfect." A lazy day spent in bed and bath, ordering room service? Oh, yeah.

"Doesn't it? You. Me. Touching. Water. Food."

"It does." Ryan pulled free so he could get rid of the condom, but he didn't move far. He knew Bleu needed touch right now, connection.

He hoped Bleu needed him.

That was the only way this was going to end like he wanted it to. With them together.

Chapter Eleven

"GOD, you were right." Ryan sounded like sex made flesh.

Bleu licked his fingers clean. "About what?" He loved being right.

"This flatbread. It's better than sex."

Bleu reached over, pinched one of Ryan's nipples unerringly. "Better than?"

They'd had a glorious day thus far—napping and bathing, listening to *Sherlock* for a few episodes before ordering food. This was like heaven with sex.

"Well, as good as, with the right person." Ryan laughed for him but didn't pull away from the touch.

"Fair enough. I love the onions best. They're almost like candy."

"They are!" Ryan sounded so surprised. And pleased.

"What all do you have to do this week? More teaching?"

"Not a lot. I have a snowboard exhibition Saturday, but then I'll be back for the party."

God, he would like to experience that—to be able to watch. He couldn't, and wishing for it didn't do a damn bit of good. "That's cool. I'm going to go out snowmobiling, I think."

"Oh, babe, that sounds too cool." Ryan stroked his cheek.

"I like to try new things. Stoney says it's so fun to go fast."

"It is. Is he driving?" Ryan didn't sound worried, more curious.

"I assume so. I don't know that he'd let me do it…."

Ryan laughed softly. "I just meant no one else was taking you out. Stoney is taken, so I trust him."

"Stoney is the most married, and I'm really good at knowing who I'm sleeping with." He poked Ryan's ribs. "I wouldn't have flirted with you if I was still with Dan."

"I know. I was just…." Ryan paused. "I was jealous."

"We haven't been lovers for a long time. I'm not sure we ever were, not really."

"No? I think that about Phil too. Is that bad?"

He had to think about that a second, but not long. "I think it's better. I was going to marry Dan."

"Was it just comfortable?"

"Yeah. I-I like him, he likes me, and we had a nice time. He's everything you could ask for—kind, sweet, well-off. I like his house, everything, but…." But there wasn't any passion. He went to bed every night with his best friend, but that was all. Add to that Dan's constant worry, and finally he couldn't do it anymore.

"Phil was all business." Ryan snorted a little. "I thought it was something real, but I think he just wanted to be able to watch what I ate."

"Why?" He didn't understand. "You're beautiful, not to mention that you're not competing anymore."

"His company managed me. Still does, when it comes to event appearances. The design stuff I handle myself."

"Will you show me one day? The designs?" He couldn't pretend not to get it. He counted on the sales from Dan's studio, or he had back at the beginning.

"I will. I want to show you everything."

"Okay. I want to know." He craved input, especially from anyone daring to be his lover.

"Good." Ryan slid his chair around the table a little, then fed him another bite of flatbread. It was spicy and just right, making his eyes cross. "God, I love to watch you eat."

He remembered that too, from back in the day.

"It's not gross?" He worried that he had stuff in his teeth.

"Not even a little," Ryan murmured. "Sexy. I don't understand how anyone wouldn't say so."

Bleu's cheeks began to heat, and he grinned, ducked his head.

"No hiding, babe. Not even for good things."

"I don't!"

"You try, but there's no need." Ryan tucked Bleu's hair back behind his ear. "I like all your expressions."

"Everyone says I have no poker face."

"It's true. I can read it all."

That could be dangerous. Bleu decided he liked that idea. A little danger. Especially when Ryan was the one he was courting it with.

"Like here." Ryan traced his forehead. "You have lines here showing you're thinking."

"Yeah? Can you tell what?" Bleu frowned mightily.

Ryan chuckled softly. "That you're trying hard not to let me know what you're thinking."

"Butthead."

"It's true." Ryan petted his cheeks. "You don't have to run from me."

God, that made tingles slide up and down his spine, made his breath catch in his chest. Ryan was just—well, all grown-up Ryan was something else entirely from college Ryan.

"I want to relearn everything about you. I want to be able to…." Ryan chuckled softly. "I want a lot."

"I have a lot to give." That he knew. He had a career, he had a life, and he was damn good in bed, right?

Maybe it was silly to be talking long-term, but hope was a good thing.

"You do. I can't believe how much you've changed and how much you've stayed the same, all at once."

"I feel that way too. You're Ryan but—more?" He leaned, and Ryan was right there to hold him. He knew Ryan had a whole life in Boulder, that the party would come and go and they'd be separated again, but right now it didn't matter.

Right now Bleu was going to bask in the glow of this little fantasy.

He needed it. Just for a second.

"Stop stressing. Please. I'm right here."

"I know. I just keep thinking how bad I am at this."

"At what?" Ryan took his hand.

"Needing. I don't want you to think I'm needy."

"I don't." Ryan laughed. "Well, I hope you're needy in some ways, though."

"That's wanton, I think. Maybe hungry."

"Definitely. You said we got to spend the whole day…."

"I have no plans today." None but exploring Ryan's body.

"Well, see there? We're gonna have a ball."

"A ball?" He let himself sound as lecherous as a villain tying a lady to a train track.

"Mmm. Or three or four."

"Yeah." He nodded, smiled, and then stretched all along Ry, rubbing.

"I say we move back to the bed…." Ryan rose, dragging him up.

"I do like how you think."

"Me too." Ryan kissed him lightly. "More privacy."

"Yes." He and Dan might be broken up, but that would still be weird as all get-out. No matter how good Dan's Aspen booty call, he didn't deserve to walk in on what they had planned.

Because they had a lot planned.

Chapter Twelve

RYAN was lying in the bed, watching Bleu sleep after their postsupper orgasm. This was the best day ever. Seriously.

He was loose and relaxed and happy as a clam.

Which was, naturally, when his phone rang.

He grabbed it, scowling when he saw Phil's name. "What?"

"Wow, nice greeting. Where are you? You're supposed to be at the Tarlington Snow Inc. meet and greet here at the barn."

"Shit. Seriously? I thought that was tomorrow morning."

"No, that's the neoprene guys."

"Fuck. I'll be there in… fifteen?"

"Are you tomcatting around?" Phil was never going to let him live this down.

"No. I'm with Bleu. I honestly thought I was clear until tomorrow." He had to go bathe real quick, and dress.

"I'll make excuses. Hurry."

"Thanks, man." He hung up, then bent to kiss Bleu. "Hey, babe, I suck. I have an event here at the barn. You're welcome to come, but I need to go get dressed."

"Go. Go, I need to spend some time with Floyd. I've neglected him."

"I'll holler when it's done." Even if Bleu was done for the night, he wanted to just let Bleu know he wanted to call, just to touch base.

"Cool. I might order some late night goodies to share, a pot of coffee…."

"I would love that. It won't be more than an hour or two." The Tarlington guys were all business, even at parties.

"Good deal." Bleu lifted his face for a quick kiss. "Enjoy yourself."

He kissed that mouth nice and hard, leaving it a little swollen and bruised. "Have fun with Floyd." Then he had to run for it, tugging on his clothes before heading out through the sitting area. "Oh, hey, Dan."

One eyebrow winged up. "Hello, Ryan. What a… pleasant surprise."

"Yeah. Sorry, I gotta run. Spaced an event." Truthfully, he thought Phil had just made a spot for him in this one today. He'd triple-checked his schedule.

"Oh… all right. I'll see if Bleu needs anything."

"You might knock." Not that Bleu wouldn't have heard them. He waved before heading out, feeling even worse now, because he was leaving Bleu to deal with Dan.

He did his walk—hell, his run—of shame and ducked into the shower as soon as he stripped down. God, he hoped no one noticed.

The whole main ranch area seemed to be rocking. Sleigh rides and hot chocolate. When he went back out there, his wet hair tucked under a little knit cap, no one teased or accosted him, so he figured he'd done all right.

Phil was holding court when he walked in, telling wild stories about different athletes' exploits. He was always in his element like this, and Ryan wasn't. He just wasn't.

"Here he is! Ryan Shields, at your service."

The temptation to curtsey was huge. He manfully resisted. "Hey, folks."

About ten beautiful lumberjackual men surrounded him, pouring testosterone from every pore. Lord. Maybe he still smelled like sex.

He shook hands and gave everyone his very best smile. *Be charming. Praise the product. Give everyone a thumbs-up.*

Ryan felt a little like chum in shark-infested waters. Too bad his own personal hammerhead was waiting in his cabin.

Lord. He just blinked and tried to work through the change of pace from Bleu and the fun they were having.

"Everything okay, babe?" Phil handed him a sparkling water.

"Huh? Yeah. Yeah, this was just totally off the grid for me. I thought sure I had checked my schedule."

"I added it the other day. There was an opening in your schedule, and I knew you'd want to meet these guys."

"I do. Point me toward our rep, and I'll make nice." No, he had checked his schedule at about 9:00 a.m., but he wasn't going to argue that now. Phil had probably agreed to the party "the other day." He'd just neglected to tell Ryan.

That was one reason they'd never worked out. Phil wanted to control and schedule every second of his life. He liked to be able to slide from one thing to another, to work when a burst of creativity hit him.

"Mike. The big beautiful redhead with the beard. He's the account holder."

"Thanks." He ducked away, heading for the mountain of a man with the infectious grin. "Hey, Mike? I'm Ryan. Phil says you're to thank for getting my designs into production with you guys."

"I am." Ryan's hand was swallowed in one of Mike's. Damn. "I'm damn pleased to be able to say I've met you."

"Same here. You really went to bat for me." He'd heard about the negotiations with the owners.

"Well, I have to admit, I'm a fan."

"Yeah? That's awesome. Thank you." He liked the guy already.

"You're welcome. So, have you come up this way often?"

"I've been up a few times. I love this place, you know? It has all the outdoor sports and all the love."

"Yeah. I love the idea of a rainbow-friendly place." Mike beamed at him. "It's so nice when everyone is family."

"Right?" He could have liked Mike a lot, in a lot of ways, but now there was Bleu again. "So, is there anything you guys need from me this weekend?"

"Do you have a date for the party Saturday night?"

"I think I do. Can I be super honest?"

"Ah, you're taken, right? Of course you are." Mike grinned sheepishly. "I can't be blamed for trying."

"Well, the thing is, I just met up with an ex of mine, and we hit it off again. So I hope he'll be my date, but if fate hadn't stepped in, I totally would have been all over you." He smiled, really meaning it. "Have you met Geoff? The chef behind all this amazing food?" Geoff deserved a shot at a hookup.

"I haven't. I just arrived. I am staying in the single cabin, though. In case magic happens."

"Well, a lot of the guys around here are magical. Good luck, man." He held out one hand, and Mike shook again. "And I hope we can be friends."

That was good business, after all.

"I would love that. I really have watched you for a lot of years."

"That rocks, man. I appreciate that. Do you shred?"

"I'm a skier, more than anything. Snowshoes too."

"Oh, man, I haven't snowshoed in years. That's a workout."

They got to talking about snowshoeing, and yeah, he could be friends with Mike, no problem. The guy was smart, had some great ideas for innovations, and was far more involved in the snow sport business than just a salesman would be. They exchanged numbers, just so they could touch base.

"Hopefully I'll see you around. I'm going to be at the exhibition."

"Excellent!" He shook hands again. "I might stay a few extra days. Think about it. We can snowshoe."

"Yeah? I'll see what I can swing. I'd love to show you a couple of tricks."

"That would be so cool." They grinned and smacked each other on the back, and Ryan moved on. He ducked Phil to check in with Alan Grey, who was an old competitor. If the owners were in from Vermont, Mike would have introduced him. So he figured he was safe. He was off the hook soon.

"Hey, man. Can we get the hell out of Dodge soon?" Alan looked a little wild around the edges.

"You know it. Where's the man?"

Alan grimaced. "He stayed at the cabin. Said he might be coming down with something. Liar. He came down with a great big urge to watch Food Network."

"Mine said he needed to play with the dog."

"Bastards." Alan glanced around. "Come on. There's another way out."

"Yeah?" He nodded, and they used the bluster of the waiters as a cover to sneak out into the space between the smaller convention space and one of the barns. "Dude, you rock."

"I know. Look, I want to chat tomorrow, but I really need to go beat some butt right now."

"TMI."

"Yeah, yeah. He ditched me for Guy Fucking Fieri."

"Oops." He clapped Alan on the back. "Night." He checked his watch. Only an hour. Yay.

He found Floyd out in the little dog run, Dan and Bleu standing out there, Bleu's face like a thundercloud.

"…don't want you to do it. It's dangerous. I'm worried about you. We're still worried about you, you know. You don't have anything to prove."

Uh, whoa. Ryan cleared his throat. "I saw Floyd and came to see if he wanted to play ball."

"Hey, Ry." Bleu's face lit up. "If you can find it under all the snow. He's being stubborn."

Ryan wasn't sure whether Bleu meant Floyd or Dan.

"Okay." He slid between them to give Bleu a kiss.

Bleu leaned for a second and hummed.

"Well, I'll see you later, Bleu." Dan waited a moment, then stomped off, muttering.

"Okay, so. Why is he so worried, babe?" Ryan asked.

"I'm leaving the cabin without being wrapped in Bubble Wrap?"

"But he specifically said 'don't do it.'" Ryan wanted to know who the "we" were too.

"Oh, I'm supposed to go with Stoney on the snowmobile Saturday. I could fall off, a bear could attack. Hell, a yeti could show up, seduce Stoney, and leave me stranded."

"Yodelayheehoo." He blinked when Floyd tipped up his nose and howled. "You sure he's not a Saint Bernard?"

"Nope. Anything is possible. How was your party?"

"It was endless. I met a nice sales rep, though. I'm going to try to hook him up with Geoff for a night of amazing antics."

"Yeah? Geoff needs ten or twelve orgasms."

"Right? Is Floyd ready to go in, babe? It's freezing." They didn't need to be all icy.

"I think so. I didn't want to be lectured. I hoped coming out here would derail him."

"Ah. Good thought, bad execution. He's probably waiting for you in the cabin too. Phil is just peeved enough to interrupt at mine too. Want to go to the great room at the house? We can beg for our nighttime snacks." They'd had super fancy nibbles and booze at the party. He'd refrained.

"Sounds perfect. We can find a quiet corner out of the way of all the hustle and bustle."

"Sounds fab. Do I need to help with Floyd?"

"Nope. Floyd. Come." Bleu moved to the gate of the run and opened it easily, Floyd trotting right to Bleu. Bleu attached the harness again, and boom. They were on their way.

He liked this—wandering in the snow, Bleu on his arm. The main house looked warm and inviting, the lights pouring out onto the frost. They slid in through the foyer like ghosts, wanting a two-seater not too far from the fire. The smell of mulled cider hit them, as well as hot chocolate.

"It smells like winter in here, you know? Not like Christmas, but like winter."

"I think so too." Ryan took a deep breath, his eyes closed. Bleu had taught him that. Take away the view, concentrate on the touch or scent.

Bleu's fingers brushed his cheeks, watching him. "I love the apple-cinnamon smell the best, but the chocolate's not bad at all."

"Well, let's find a seat, and I'll get us both a cup of cider." He loved how people here were so much more casual than at the big ski parties. This was where couples were gravitating, where people played board games.

"Is there a love seat or something?"

"There's this one right near the fire. Is that too warm?"

Bleu shook his head. "Works for me."

Yeah, poor baby had been out there who knew how long with Dan. He steered Bleu toward the love seat, and they sank down, Floyd plopping onto the floor, nose toward the fire.

"Oh, isn't that lovely?" Bleu leaned toward the fire.

"It is. The fireplace is this big thing. Have you felt the big carved mantel? It's got deer and aspen trees and stuff."

"No. Show me."

God, that made him smile. He loved how Bleu needed to experience things, to "see" things.

"Okay, here." He helped Bleu around Floyd, who never moved, and off to the side of the fireplace. "Okay, don't get too close to the center, as it's really hot." Ryan placed Bleu's hands on the amazing carved piece. Bleu traced the shapes, one after another.

"This is a tree. What's this?"

"A deer."

"Are they smaller than horses?"

"Yep. They're like really leggy dogs, and they have antlers, or branched horns."

"Huh. Neat." Bleu explored the deer, face utterly fascinated.

Why hadn't anyone done stuff like this with Bleu? Hell, Ryan was making mental notes now about finding a petting zoo so Bleu could feel all the different animals.

"Is there more to look at?" Bleu followed the mantel. "This is a star? A sun?"

"It's a star. The sun is a little high up for us to feel right now. Here's a squirrel. They have a lot of mantels like this in Germany and Switzerland." Ryan pushed Bleu gently to touch the squirrel's tail.

"It's rough!"

"That's just how it was carved."

Bleu nodded. "That's what I thought. It's hard to do fuzzy in wood. Clay is easier."

"Is it? Because it starts out wet and soft?" He wanted to know all about what Bleu did. He knew Bleu had done it in college, but his stuff now was light-years away from that. Hell, Bleu had done everything in the art building while he was skiing. They had been wild lovers, but somehow, they hadn't been friends.

"It's malleable. I mean, you can't push wood around with your fingers, right? You have to use chisels and saws. I'd hurt myself. I have a friend that does woodwork. Nat. His hands feel like a Frankenstein."

"Ouch. I know an ice sculptor. He starts with a chainsaw."

"Yeah? I liked the snow. Sand is cool too. I can imagine that ice sculpting is a little intense."

"Is it weird to know it will just dissolve?"

"Not for me. Once the work is over, it's over. Even in clay, once it's cast, it's done for me. I never really connect with it again."

"Huh." Ryan kinda got that. His work had been fleeting for so many years. The design stuff he got to touch and see, but the boarding was nothing but air and trophies he rarely looked at.

"Is that weird to you?" Bleu asked.

"No. No, in fact I think I really get that." Ryan chuckled. "I'm the king of seconds in the air, remember."

"I know. I mean, I don't, but I try to. Sometimes I feel like the world is an elephant, like in the story."

"I bet." He took Bleu's hands in his and squeezed. "Want some cider?"

"I do, thanks." Bleu nodded and moved toward the seat they'd picked out.

He made sure Bleu was safely around Floyd before he said, "Be right back." He headed for the drink and snack station.

There were a couple of men standing around, flirting with each other madly. No question that they were going to bed together. Ryan grinned, thinking of Mike and hoping he got lucky too.

He poured two ciders from the big silver coffee server, then garnished them with the orange slices and sugar cubes sitting nearby. There were nibbles too, so Ryan began building a plate.

"You slipped out of the party. Naughty, naughty." Phil stole a cookie from his plate. "Is that him? Are you going to introduce me?"

"What?" Phil caught him flat-footed, making him scramble. "I met with the rep, man."

"He was very taken with you. Very. You did good. I'm just giving you shit."

"Thanks." He was avoiding introducing Phil to Bleu, which wasn't fair. "Come on, hon. You need to meet Bleu."

"I'd love to." Phil smiled at him, winked. "I need to see who's won your heart."

"Yeah, yeah." He carried cups over, balancing them with a plate of food, laughing when Floyd's tail thumped on the floor. "Bleu? I have someone for you to meet. This is Phil. Phil, Bleu."

Bleu smiled up and held out one hand, nowhere near Phil. "Hey, there."

Phil glanced at him with a hint of panic and, at his nod, leaned over and shook Bleu's hand. "Pleased to meet you."

"Same with you. Would you like to join us?"

Ack. Please let Phil say no.

"Sure. Let me pull up a chair."

He glared at Phil, who gave him a beatific smile. *Oh, fucker. Prurient fucker.*

"Cool." Bleu's face said something else, so he took Bleu's hand to give him the cider.

"I got munchies too," Ryan said.

"Yeah? What is there?" Bleu's eyes moved so fast, like he was always searching. He hated the weight of glasses on his face, and he used to say that hiding his eyes was for other people's comfort, not his.

"Bacon things with puff pastry and cheese. Jalapeno poppers, kinda. Sliced ones. Uh, crab puffs? And artichoke dip on english muffin triangles." Geoff was putting it out there.

"Oh damn. That sounds amazing. Geoff must be in heaven." Bleu's laugh made him feel a little like they were the only two men on earth.

"I bet he is. He loves bizarre appetizers." The man loved little desserts too, so he would bet they appeared soon. Tiny was also pastry obsessed. It was adorable.

"Here we go," Phil said, scraping up a chair.

Bleu sipped his cider, eyes closed now as he focused. Ryan wanted to know what Bleu tasted, wanted to know what Bleu tasted like after his drink. Would it be tart, cinnamony, spicy? All of the above?

Phil was watching him when he glanced up, and he grinned a little. He didn't want Phil to feel bad, but Ryan refused to hide how he felt.

"Man, if you'd looked at me like that once in all the time we were dating, I'd have been lost."

Bleu blinked, trying to look at something, maybe him.

Ryan just tried to laugh it off some. "We're just very different folks, Phil."

Bleu tilted his head, obviously intrigued. "How does he look at me?"

Phil glanced at Ryan again, then grinned widely. "Like you're a steep slope of brand-new powder on Christmas morning."

Ryan was going to punch Phil right in the face. The one thing he had on Bleu was that, while the amazing son of bitch could feel him tense, could hear any little nuance in his voice, he couldn't see his face.

Bleu's cheeks went pink, which was sweet, but he was still going to punch Phil in the balls. Just as he was about to invite Phil to leave, though, Mike from Tarlington came trotting over.

"There you are! Ryan, can you come sign a board for me? We brought some in for the exhibition, and the brass think it would be a great giveaway." Mike danced from foot to foot.

"Uh…."

"Go on, Ry. We're cool. Seriously. I promise not to wheedle any secrets from your ex." Bleu grinned at him, wicked as anything.

"Uh-huh. You're both buttheads." He rose, nodding to Mike. "I'm happy to help. Point me to the board."

"It's on display at the party. It'll just take a minute."

He hated leaving Phil alone with Bleu, but business was business, right?

Right. And Bleu wasn't helpless, was he? No.

Although, that wasn't really what he was worried about.

No, what he worried about was Phil and Bleu telling stories on him. Bad ones or good ones. He wanted to find his own footing in this new… thing he and Bleu had, for want of a better word.

He wanted to start over, and he fully intended to have the ending of this story be different this time.

Mike led him away, showing him off a little when they walked back into the party. He nodded at the right times, stood for the photo op while he signed the snowboard with a Sharpie.

His head was in there with Bleu, though. No question.

"Huh?" He shook his head to clear it, then met Mike's eyes. "I'm sorry, what?"

"Would you mind meeting an investor? Two minutes."

"Sure. Two minutes." This was a business trip, after all. He would have to be firm after that, though. Bleu was sitting by a fireplace, waiting to be with him, and he wanted that too.

Maybe even needed it.

BLEU curled his feet underneath him and smiled in Phil's direction. "It's good to meet you. I'm sorry I was in a hurry the night you came up. I had been without Floyd here all day."

"No problem. I was a little, uh, forceful," Phil said, snorting a little. He sounded pretty wry.

"Yeah, Ry explained. I'd apologize, but I'm not sorry that y'all didn't hook up."

"I am, but I can live with it."

He had to smile at the humor in Phil's voice. The guy had a good handle on laughing at himself, Bleu thought.

"So how did y'all meet? Through work?"

"Yeah. He needed better management. Someone to handle all his sponsors. I saw his potential."

"Good for you. For both of you, really." Bleu didn't have to worry about sponsors, at least not in the same way. He had commissions, and half the money came up front.

He never lacked for clients. In fact, he often turned people down. A project had to sing to him.

Bleu was beginning to itch to get into the clay anyway. He wanted to start creating faces, to feel the way the clay slid, the throb of the music. All of it.

"Bleu?"

"Hmm?"

"You were somewhere far away, huh?"

"I must have been. Sorry."

Phil just laughed some more. "You know he travels just as much as he used to, right?"

He wasn't sure what that meant. Ry had traveled with the ski team, that was it.

"He does all sorts of engagements now, and has a full schedule. How much time will he have?"

"For what?" He didn't follow. He hadn't asked Ry for anything.

"For a blind man. I'm not trying to be ugly, Bleu, but you know there's a lot of moving parts involved in your life."

"So what is it like when you're trying, honey?" He didn't need this shit. He hadn't asked Ryan for a commitment, help, not a *thing*.

"Oh, I'm a corporate shark. I can be awful."

"I try not to be. I'm an artist, so I have a lot of time where I'm in my studio with music for company."

"That sounds soothing." Phil leaned forward, the air shifting around them. "I'm just saying he might not be any better suited to taking care of you than he used to be."

"Ah." Figured that was what Ryan had told Phil about him. "I don't need taking care of. I've done fine for almost a decade."

"Right. I know I probably sound like a jealous ex, but really I'm Ryan's friend."

"And partly his business manager. I can see where you'd want to protect your investment."

"Ouch. But okay, that could be part of it."

"I don't intend to make him my caregiver, don't worry. I'm fairly sure he didn't apply for the job either."

Bleu went for dry, and he felt like he did a fairly good job of it.

"No, no, I'm sure not. Look, I know it's none of my business, but that's never stopped me before. I stick my nose in."

"Fair enough." He wanted Ryan to come back so Phil would shut up and go away. He thought about getting up and leaving, but that felt like retreat, like surrendering.

He was tired of people assuming he would give up on anything just because he was blind. Including Ryan.

"Hey! Bleu. Uh, Phil, can I borrow Bleu? I need to chat with him about the party."

Bleu took a second to place Ford's voice, which meant he was pretty rattled.

"Sure you can. See you, Phil. Floyd, come."

Floyd came right to him, nails clicking on the hardwood floor. He grabbed the harness and rose, following Ford to the kitchen.

He didn't say anything on the trip, because he knew the piece he'd done was a surprise for Stoney, and he needed Ford to tell him when it was all clear.

"Okay, we're safe. I overheard a few words there, and I wanted you to know. Phil and Ryan have been broken up for, like, six months."

"Yeah, Ryan told me. I'm guessing Phil regrets it, huh?" He could see that too. He'd regretted leaving Ry for a long time. He knew it had been the right decision, though. He'd been young and scared; Ry had been flying up the ladder of his career and needed his freedom.

"I think he's just worried. Stoney tells me he showed up expecting a booty call, but he's not a bad guy. Socially awkward…." Ford laughed, which invited him to chuckle too.

"Yeah, I get that." He guessed. Really, he didn't. He just wanted to get to know Ryan again.

"Well, I thought I would help out. I hope I didn't make things worse."

"Why would you? I needed rescuing. That was getting a little awkward."

"Yeah, and you were kinda stuck."

"Stuck to what?" Geoff bustled in from the back door, a gust of cold air coming with him.

"The leather couch. It's cold out there, huh?" See him, see him make small talk.

"It is. My chest is trying to cave in. Weren't you with Ryan?"

"He had to run do a couple things with a sponsor."

"Oh. Well, have a sit. Coffee or tea? Coke?"

"Geoff, I know you're busy. You don't have to wait on me."

"Stop it. I love having you."

"Dr Pepper, please." There was no arguing with Geoff. None.

"You got it. Ah, Tiny, those two trays to the Tarlington party."

"You got it, Geoff."

That was where Ry was, he thought. The Tarlington party.

"If you see Ryan, can you tell him I'm in the kitchen?" He'd wait for a while. The kitchen was warm and smelled so good.

"You know it." Tiny's rough voice was always so kind. He loved the way it almost echoed in his chest, the low rumble.

Geoff set his Dr Pepper in front of him. "So what happened? Ford slipped out, so you can tell me."

"Oh, Ry's ex was warning me off. No big. Just weird and uncomfortable, you know?" Especially since Ryan hadn't seemed terribly concerned about Phil.

"Did he write you a check? I would totally cash it if he wrote you a check."

"No… should I have asked? That would be cool."

"Right?" Geoff laughed. "I mean, you wouldn't do what he wanted. You could just split it with Ryan."

"Hell, I'd donate it to Quartz's college fund for watching the dog."

"I like it. Don't worry on Quartz, though. Ford has him covered."

"Oh, I have no doubt. They're good people."

"Yeah." A chair scraped out, and Geoff sat down. "Oh, that feels good."

"You been working your hiney off, buddy?" Like Geoff ever had downtime. Ever. He was like the Energizer Bunny.

"I have! The party Saturday is the big culmination, though. Then I'm back to making dinner for family and guests and cooking a lot of bacon in the mornings."

"What do you have to make for the party? Just tons of nibbles or do you have a plated meal?"

"Nibbles. They wanted a Mexican feast, so I get to do street tacos and slaw, nachos Texas style, and I'm making these Mexican rice cakes. A churro bar. And Tiny is doing a meat station."

"Oh… yum. Yum. Seat me near the nachos." He missed Texas-style nachos like a sore tooth. The ones up here and in New Mexico were fine, but sometimes a man just wanted a tortilla quarter with meat, beans, and broiled cheese.

"Totally. Anytime you want Tex-Mex, Stoney has instructed me on how to make it." Geoff said it fondly.

"It's funny how you never get over wanting it. Is it weird to cook meat when you don't eat it?"

"Nope. It's easier now that I have Tiny to taste, but I try hard to live and let live. It helps that Stoney works hard to have responsibly raised meat, and if he kills game, we use every bit of it. He doesn't allow trophy hunting on the ranch."

"That makes sense. You're a good guy, man. I'm glad to call you friend."

"You know, I never thought I'd make so many good friends, but here at the ranch? It's like magic for me." Geoff touched his hand. "I love it here."

"Me too." He beamed, or hoped so. Maybe he looked like a scary skeleton.

"Hey, babe. There you are." Ryan kissed the top of his head. "Can I sit a minute and hide, Geoff?"

"Of course. This seems to be the place for finding peace in this house."

"It does." Ryan sat next to him, then took his hand. "Sorry, babe. I got there and everyone wanted something."

"I've been there. Gallery openings can be like that." He wasn't pissed off. A little sad, maybe, because Phil had been so "back off Ryan," but not mad.

"You okay?"

He heard what Ryan was asking, which was "was Phil a shit" or something like that.

"I'm good. Phil wants me to know that you're not going to be able to take care of me." Petty? Maybe, but it was still true.

"Oh God. Babe, he asked me why we broke up, and I told him how I freaked out. We're both different now. He's just not very subtle. Sorry."

"No worries. He's got to protect his investment in you, right?"

"Argh. Yes. That makes me nuts." Ryan squeezed his hand. "It smells great, Geoff. Whatever it is."

Geoff hooted. "It is finger foods. For you."

"For me?" Ryan asked. "Was I hungry?"

"If Geoff cooks for you, you must be hungry, Ry."

"Well, okay. You'll have to help me, babe. There's a lot."

"Is this for a party, Geoff? I mean, is the family coming?"

"Stoney and Ford will be in, and Tiny and Tanner and Doogie. Maybe Angie and Hetty."

"Ah, so we get to be part of the family." He liked that bit. He liked believing it.

"You do. I think it works."

"Me too." That was Stoney, who was yawning as he said the words. "They're winding down finally. The big parties. The runners will clean up."

"I have goodies for them too," Geoff murmured.

"Good man. I have to say, those kids are busting their asses. I'm damn pleased." Stoney plopped down beside him. "Hey, Bleu. Ryan."

"Hey, man." The sound of a plate being pushed came to him as Ryan spoke. "Have a snack."

"Oh, poppers! I love these. You tried them yet, Bleu? They taste like home—bacon and everything."

"I haven't. Ryan made up a plate, but I never got one."

"I'll hook you up, then. Ryan? You want one?"

"Please."

"Plates," Geoff said, plonking something on the table. Plates, he presumed.

"Sit, Geoff. Time for you to rest."

"Rest? What's that? We never rest around here except in the spring."

"Hush. The worst is over, and Tiny is out there pushing the leftovers on guests like a fiend." That was Ford, plopping down too. The noises were so fascinating.

"Spring is bad for business?"

Ford grunted. "Too cold for outdoorsy stuff, too mushy for winter sports. A couple of families come up and do hot tubbing, but that's it."

"Mushy." Bleu liked that word.

"Yep. The ground likes to suck your boots off," Stoney said.

"Ew!" And also damn cool. How neat was that?

Ryan snorted, making Bleu grin with the sarcasm in the wordless sound. "Oh, I used to hate March and April on the competition circuit. People still tried to have events, and we all ended up buttpassing and wiping out because the surface was bad."

"Buttpassing?" Bleu asked.

"Falling and sliding on our asses," Ryan said.

"Does that hurt?"

"Sometimes. Depends on the surface. If there's a lot of ice and rocks mixed in, yeah."

"No rocks in your butt, Ry. It's perfect as is."

"Thank you."

"Ew." Geoff was right there, and he thought maybe the man was having a snack.

"What? It is perfect!"

"Sorry, Bleu. Stoney's is perfect," Ford pointed out.

"I've never felt Stoney's, but I assume it's a cowboy butt. I like snowboarder butt." It seemed like a perfect explanation.

"Well, I'm not going to let you feel up Stoney's backside, man. We'll just have to agree to disagree."

"Fair enough." He started laughing, and Ryan and Stoney joined right on in.

"You guys suck. I have no perfect asses," Geoff complained.

"Have you met Mike? He's a rep for the snow sports group having the party. Big redhead." Ryan sounded gleeful. "Sweet guy. Snowshoer. Lives in Telluride."

"No." Geoff's voice took on a hopeful tone. "I need to go retrieve some trays."

"You should introduce them, Ry. If he seems good."

"He seems like a great guy. You have to come with me so I don't get stalled again. Then we can come back for munchies."

"Save me a seat, guys?"

"Always, Bleu." Stoney sounded like he was damn near asleep in his chair.

They would be lucky if Stoney wasn't in bed when they got back.

"Floyd. Come." Floyd hopped up. Ryan helped him into his coat, which he thought he'd left in the great room. "Onward, Geoff and Ryan."

"Do you feel a little like a reindeer, Geoff?"

"A touch, yeah. Jingle jingle jingle."

"Mush. You're huskies."

They all laughed, but Ryan took the arm not holding Floyd, and they set out into the frigid night to hook Geoff up. That was hysterical.

"Geoff?" That was Tiny. "Everything okay?"

"Fine. Going to drop off trays, get an introduction maybe."

"Oh-ho! Okay, well, I'll be back at the kitchen. This crew is eaten out, I think."

"Well, I'll drop these off, just to make sure."

"The kids will nosh if nothing else."

He thought Tiny meant the runners, who were all older teenagers and college students.

"Cool. Thanks. Ryan? Is he here?"

"Uh-huh. Come on. Mike? You got a minute?"

"I do."

Oh, deep voice, husky. Interesting. He'd not gotten to meet the man when he whisked Ryan away.

"I wanted to introduce my fella, Bleu, and this is Geoff. I told you about him."

Bleu held out a hand to shake, and the grip was strong, big, but not brutal.

"Hi, Bleu." Mike let go. "Geoff, pleased to meet you."

"I…. Hello."

Dude. Listen to that. That was real interest. Like whoa.

"Um, do you have a few minutes to chat? I loved the food." Mike sounded downright tickled. And also interested.

"Did you? What was your favorite?"

Bleu was trying hard not to giggle.

"The jalapenos. I love spice." Their voices moved away.

"Wow, I guess we really were just here to facilitate," Ryan murmured.

"That was super cool, man. You're like the queer guy whisperer."

"I totally am. Now, if I can just get Dan to go sleep with Phil, we could have a cabin to ourselves."

"Oh, wouldn't that be nice? I mean, you're welcome to stay in my room, but it's not alone." And Dan didn't approve of him having a life.

"I know, and Dan has been weird…. Back to the kitchen for now?"

"Dan was born weird. Yes, please."

"Let's go. Floyd with us?"

"He is."

They headed off to the kitchen, where the cowboys were all assembled now.

"Hey! Come sit down, guys." That voice was less familiar, but he figured out it was Tanner before he embarrassed himself.

"Hey. Geoff's having a discussion with one of my sponsors."

Bleu let Ryan lead him to a seat, get him settled.

"Cool!" Tiny chuckled warmly. "Geoff could use some time out of the kitchen."

"That was what I was thinking. A nice, happy lumberjack that needs a friend with bennies."

Bleu personally thought that Geoff needed something way more intense than a friend with benefits, but what did he know?

Tanner snorted. "I am the only straight man at the Leanin' N."

"Quartz is very interested in the idea of girls, when he's not stressing their cooties. One day you'll be one of two."

"I like the ladies." That came from… Angie? She was a wrangler too, he thought.

"You better only like one."

He didn't know that voice.

"Bleu, Ryan, this is Hetty, Angie's wife and one of our offsite horse breeders. She's our sleigh horse source." Stoney was laughing, and that merriment made Bleu smile.

"Oh, I'd like to take a sleigh ride one day. Ryan told me all about them."

"Anytime," Hetty said. "I've got some lazy porkers who need exercise."

"You mean you're breeding sled pigs now?" Ford teased.

"Sled pigs…." Bacon in a harness. Good Lord.

"Oink!" That was Doogie, his old smoker voice clear.

"I'm considering just giving you guys llamas from now on."

"Or ostriches!" Angie slapped the table with a bang.

"Oh God no." Stoney hooted. "Ostriches are only good for boots."

"I've touched ostrich eggs before. They don't feel real. They feel like they've been carved."

"They so do." That was Tiny.

This was so much fun. It reminded him of family get-togethers in Texas. All talk, all bluster and teasing.

And they didn't act like he didn't belong.

"The yolks are super fragile, I guess," Stoney added.

And then Ford asked, "How do you know?"

"*Chopped*."

"Oh, I like that one!" They explained everything that was happening so you could just listen.

"Right?" Stoney poked his arm gently. "They've got shit on that show I would never put in my mouth."

"Coward." Tiny gently touched his shoulder. "Dr Pepper again, or something warm?"

"Oh, did my drink go missing?"

"I drank it," Tanner said sheepishly.

"No worries. I'll take a cup of coffee this time. Ry? You want anything?"

"Oh, man, I would love a cup of tea. Can we help, Tiny? What can we do?"

We. A little glow filled him, because Ryan meant them. Bleu and Ryan. That he could help too.

"Sit. Visit. Eat some of this food so I don't have to put it away."

"We can so do that." Bleu had to laugh, because he'd had at least two plates of uneaten nibbles today. Now he would eat.

"What do you want, guys? Pizza rolls just came out of the oven."

"Poppers and pizza rolls!" came as a chorus.

Ryan stood, the air moving, and then Bleu smelled hot coffee. "I put just a little cream and sugar, babe."

"Thank you." He found the mug and drank deep, enjoying the bitter and sweet and creamy before the scent of tomato sauce and bacon overwhelmed everything.

Oh hell yes.

He was all over that.

"These are homemade pizza rolls," Ryan said, taking his hand to show Bleu the shape. "The other side is poppers with bacon, but I would fork that."

"Okay. Is there ranch to dip in?"

"Right here." Ryan handed him a little bowl deal.

"Cool." He used his fork for the poppers, because yeah, he would inevitably wipe his eyes or something with jalapeno fingers, and Ryan had said they were sliced, not whole.

The pizza rolls were addictive, and he found himself reaching for them, over and over. "Is there crack in these?"

"I think there's gotta be. I could eat a dozen more." Ryan was laughing, leaning close. "They're good with the ranch, even."

"Aren't they? I love ranch on anything. My palate isn't any more refined than it's ever been."

"Oh God, neither is mine. Pizza. Hamburgers. I've had sushi in Japan and fancy cheese in France, and I'm still an American snack food guy."

"I like sushi. Fancy cheese is okay if it doesn't smell like feet, but really, I'm happy with a bag of

Doritos and a Milky Way." It was okay to say that here because Geoff wasn't listening.

"Oh, I like sushi too, but here I just get spicy tuna. In Japan there's stuff you can't even imagine. Fish eggs that explode like Pop Rocks."

"No shit?" He tried to imagine fish Pop Rocks. That was… wow. Rough.

"Yeah. Here, have a bite with ranch." Ryan pressed a bite of pizza roll to his mouth.

He dared to nibble at Ryan's fingertips, just barely, just teasing. After all, Ryan knew he wasn't attached now, right?

So did everyone else, apparently.

"Ryan, what's the weirdest thing you've ever eaten, then?" Stoney asked.

"Nakji. They're baby octopus, and you eat them alive. I had them in Korea."

"Alive?" Bleu shook his head. He couldn't help it. "Don't tell Geoff."

"Never. If he was here, I would have said durian fruit."

"That smells bad. I've read about that." Bleu searched his memory. "Rotten onions, right?"

Stoney made a gagging noise.

"Kinda, yeah. It's wow. Okay, everyone else has to play."

"Mealworms," Tiny said immediately. "Steamed."

"Rocky mountain oysters." That was Stoney.

"Sweetbreads. They're fucking nasty." Angie sounded almost affronted.

"There was this hors d'oeuvres in Chicago once that was puff pastry filled with squid ink, salted cod, and raisins. I thought I would die." Ford coughed in an exaggerated way.

"Salted… and raisins?" He didn't even want to think about whatever squid ink was. He was still traumatized from when he found out honey was bee vomit.

"It tasted like really chunky black cum."

Everyone started moaning and gagging at that.

"My poor virgin ears!" he cried, flailing wildly.

"Shit. You wish." Stoney's snort made him laugh. "Do you even remember being a virgin, Bleu?"

"Nope. I was born experienced and wickedly good at this whole sex thing."

"I know better," Ryan sing-songed.

Everyone laughed, but the game went on, with stinky tofu and fermented ant eggs coming up. He couldn't imagine a better time with friends.

Sad, really, because Dan had been his best friend for a long, long time, and Bleu didn't even miss him. Somehow he needed Dan to back off the worry and get back to being… just the good guy and art fiend Bleu had first met.

He let that little pang go. Right now he was having a ball with these people that were almost like family. It was enough.

Ryan leaned close. "You going to invite me back to your cabin to spend the night, Bleu?"

"I think I am, Mr. Shields."

"Very cool." Ryan laughed, taking his hand as cowboys started to shuffle around and say good night.

"You guys need anything before I take Stoney to bed?" Ford whispered over.

Bleu thought he could hear Stoney snoring softly.

"I think we're good," Ryan said just as quietly.

"You fellas feel free to stay as long as you need to," Ford said. "Stoney. Come on, baby. Let's go to bed. Tiny's got this."

Oh, so sweet.

Ryan hummed, deep in his chest, so whatever he saw had to be as lovely as he was imagining.

"Let's sneak off too. Unless you need us, Tiny."

"Are you kidding?" Tiny kept his voice low. "I got ten kids out there desperate to earn as many hours of money as they can."

"Fair enough. Come on, Bleu. Let's go."

He nodded and found Floyd's harness. "Come on, boy."

Floyd yawned audibly. Yeah, it was past all their bedtimes. He took Ryan's arm with his other hand, feeling a great sense of… togetherness, maybe.

Whatever it was, he was going to enjoy it. Dammit.

They wandered back through the snow, and he let Floyd go to do his business before they went in.

When they made it to his cabin, Bleu was relieved that Dan was either in bed or not around. No weirdness.

They went back to the bedroom, easy as pie, both of them settling into a routine like it was nothing, like it was meant to be. The shoe was going to drop, of course it was. The party was Saturday, and then things would be over. He'd go to Santa Fe, and Ryan would go to Boulder, and they'd go to work, and things would be down to a few phone calls. Still, he could enjoy this now, couldn't he?

He let Floyd out of his harness before Ryan looped an arm around him, leading him to his bed.

Yeah. He would focus on the now. Hard.

Chapter Thirteen

RYAN woke up feeling warm and happy, just.... Yeah. Saturday was a good day. The best day.

He checked the clock. The exhibition wouldn't wait, but he had time for a nice leisurely breakfast before he had to go prepare.

Bleu had kissed him early this morning, whispering something about Floyd and snowmobiles and love before disappearing and leaving him to his dreams.

Grinning, he rolled out of bed, his everything needing stretching. First he had to hit the head, though. He made his way into the hall, looking for the bathroom.

He felt energized and ready to go, to let himself play on the pipes and show off a little bit. It was easier now, to just let it all hang out, because he wasn't worried about ruining his career.

Washing up after he did his thing, he licked his teeth. Ew. Okay, so go get cleaned up first. Then breakfast. Then event.

When he left the bathroom, though, he ran smack into Dan.

"Oops! Sorry, man. Sorry."

Dan chuckled softly. "Usually that's Bleu who smacks into me. Good morning."

"Morning. He's off snowmobiling. Is Floyd gone already?" He would walk the beast if Quartz hadn't picked him up.

"He's not here, so I'm assuming he went to doggy day care." Dan sighed. "I do wish he would have stayed home. Snowmobiles aren't safe."

He glanced at Dan before leading the way to the main room. He was glad he had pants on. "You know, he needs to experience things."

"Of course he does, but does he need to experience dangerous things? He's always trying to…. He does things I wouldn't do, and he's blind, for fuck's sake."

He couldn't even yell at the guy. Hadn't he felt unequal to the task of taking care of Bleu? The thing was, Bleu had easily learned to get along on his own. Even out here on the ranch, Bleu got around with Floyd like a champ.

"It's not like he's out there alone, Dan. I know, believe me, but he's so capable. It surprised me."

"Was he this bad before? I want to be there for him, I really do, but he just pushes me away…."

"Bad?" He paused, pondering that. "I think he's way more adventurous now. But I know he doesn't want to be a burden to anyone. If it freaks you out that he's blind, he's going to try to make things easier for you by not being around." Which was exactly what Bleu had done for him back in the day. God, he was an idiot.

"It doesn't bother me that he's blind. It bothers me that he's got a death wish, that he won't accept his limitations."

"What are his limitations?" They'd sunk down across from each other on couch and chair respectively. "I mean, why can't he ride on the back of a snowmobile or ski? He was a natural, by the way. He has as much chance as anyone of getting hurt, sure, but only as much."

"He's special. He can express things in sculpture that I can only barely understand. I want to keep that gift safe. That's reasonable, right?"

"That's sweet." How did he put this? "But I'm not sure it's okay to put him in a bubble to preserve his art, man."

God knew he'd resented Phil for watching everything he put into his mouth, for treating him like a commodity instead of a lover.

Dan sighed. "I wish I could change me, Ryan, but I can't. I know it's not fair to want to change him. It's just really complicated."

"Of course it is. You're a good friend, man. Just try hard to let him do what he wants to do, huh?" Listen to him, being all psychologist.

"Yeah. What about you? Are you a good friend? A weekend tryst? What are you to him?"

Ryan bristled, but then he took a deep breath. Dan had been perfectly open with him. He could return the favor. "I want to be a lover. Full-time. We have a lot to figure out, but I still love him."

"I love him too, but I'm not in love with him. I'm in love with his art, and he was in love with the idea of being a couple. I hope you two work out, for his sake."

Oh. Oh wow. Okay. Okay, that was… way more decent than he'd expected, and that made him a little ashamed of himself.

He smiled. "Thanks. Have you had breakfast? I need to hop in the shower, but then I'm heading to the dining room."

"I haven't, no. Do you mind company?"

"Not a bit. Meet you there in about twenty?" Dan was a part of Bleu's life. He would try to get to know the guy.

"Sounds good. I'll go grab a coffee from the lobby and give you some privacy."

"Thanks, man." He smiled, figuring they had a truce, if nothing else.

He grabbed his bag and headed into the bathroom. Light breakfast, coffee, and then he had an exhibition to do.

Then he would see about convincing Bleu to do more than let the weekend end.

Chapter Fourteen

"OH my God! It's so cool!" The world was whipping past them, the buzz of the snowmobile like a thousand angry red wasps, the vibration scary and fascinating and wonderful all at once.

Bleu was out of his mind with excitement. He clung to Stoney, feeling every bump and jump of the sled. Stoney had called it a sled.... He laughed. This was so not sledding.

This was... flying. They were flying. They hit something and the world fell out from under them for a second, and they were soaring before the snowmobile hit the ground again and they were off.

He whooped, and he felt Stoney laughing, ribs just shaking.

"You having fun, man?"

"This is amazing!" he yelled back. "Faster!"

"Hold on!" They cornered, and he had this feeling of thin air, as if they'd gone over the edge of something. Then they whipped back on a trail, the sound familiar already. "Lean left with me!"

He leaned hard, laughing loud as they cornered fast and furious. There was a loud scrape, but the sled righted, and Stoney chortled.

"You're doing great, man. You want more?"

"God yes. Please. I want to know."

"I hear you. Okay, this is tricky. We're heading down a long hill. When we hit the bottom, it will be a powdery bowl. Do exactly what I tell you, okay?"

"I will." He was great at following directions. Spectacular, even.

They stopped for just a moment, and he could feel Stoney adjusting his weight.

The sled revved up, and they began to move, the wind moving faster and faster, almost burning his cheeks with the speed of it. The incline of the snowmobile tilted sharply, and they both leaned into the drop, the icy air stealing their breath.

Bleu felt it just before the land changed, the angle trying to yank him up and back, and Stoney gunned it, pushing them straight across the bowl of powder he'd mentioned. "Lean right!"

They leaned again, spinning the sled again. He could feel the whole kit and caboodle start to sink, and Stoney hit the gas, lifting them out of the snow.

How fascinating was that? Gravity was an amazing thing.

They drove around the snow bowl a few times; then Stoney laughed and slowed down. "You about ready to go back, man? There's hot chocolate waiting for us."

"Sounds perfect."

"Cool. Okay, we have to go up the hill the other way. Remember what I told you about going up?"

"Don't lean back. I remember."

"Right. Here we go!" Stoney pushed it, the motor whining.

They headed up, and he fought gravity, his abs tight as he tried to push up the hill. They were moving real well, so he thought he was doing just fine, and Stoney wasn't tense or stressed, so yay.

This was the best thing since skiing. Seriously. "So much fun!"

"I know, right?" Stoney hollered back. "This is the best—"

A crack sounded, sharp and loud, and then it felt like they were upside down, like they were literally flying through the air, the seat of the snowmobile trying to disappear from between their legs.

The sled flipped, Stoney shouted, and Bleu lost his breath when he hit something soft and hard and freezing cold.

Then everything just… went away.

Chapter Fifteen

THE half pipe was just freaking perfect today.

Ryan tipped off the edge, swooping down one side and up the other, catching air in an easy 360 before coming back down. That gave him room for at least three more aerials on the way. He felt loose and in the zone, not having to worry about points, not having to compete against anyone.

The air made his whole face cold, even with the goggles and his hat. Man, it was freezy. He whipped back up the pipe, getting enough height to do a 450. Ryan landed it, which made the crowd cheer. He did one more big front catch aerial, not bothering to spin, before landing and slipping down to the bottom of the pipe.

Ryan pumped his arms as he crossed the finish line, snow spraying everywhere.

Hoots and hollers followed him as he unhooked his boots, and a shit-ton of folks stopped him for photo ops.

He signed everything that was thrust in front of him—skis, boards, helmets, hoodies. Ryan really wanted to get back to the ranch and see how Bleu's snowmobiling had gone, but this was his job, and he needed to do it well.

Besides, they had all of the late afternoon and the party to enjoy together.

"That was awesome, babe!" Phil came to him once he got up the hill, clapping him on the back. "You caught some amazing air!"

"It felt damn good." He grinned over. "Remind me when we're not at work to punch you in the face for trying to warn Bleu off, would you?"

"Hey! I was just trying to make things easier."

Ryan stared.

"Okay, I was being all weird, but I did have your best interests at heart."

"Weird. Bitchy. And you have to be nice from now on, okay?"

"Fine. I'll be good."

He fastened Phil with a look.

"I will. I swear. If he's what you want, go for it."

"He's who I want." No question, no hesitation.

"Good. Come on. Do the shaking hands with the bigwigs pics, and you can head out."

"I can totally do that." He liked meeting the guys, liked the fans. This was one of the good parts.

They made their way up to the VIP area, where both hot chocolate and booze was flowing. Phil introduced him to dozens of expensive-looking folks, and he caught up with a few buddies from the circuit.

So much fun. He only wished Bleu was here to experience this.

Soon. He had a few more exhibitions set in February. One in Idaho and one in Utah. Maybe he could get Bleu to go with him.

That would be fun as….

His phone buzzed in his jacket pocket, and he grabbed it. Ford Nixel. Weird.

He hit Accept. "Yo."

"Are Stoney and Bleu there with you?"

"Uh, not that I know of. I'm at the VIP right now. Did you want me to try calling Bleu?" *What the hell?*

"Can you? I can't reach Stoney, and he was supposed to be back over an hour ago."

His heart kicked into high gear. "You got it. Call you back in a minute." He moved away from the crowd, then dialed Bleu.

The ring went straight to voicemail, Bleu's voice on the line. "Hey, leave a message and I'll get right back to you."

Shit. He called Ford back, worry knotting in his belly.

"Anything?"

"No. You?"

"No. I'm going to send Tanner out to see if he can find them. There's a storm coming this afternoon, of course, because we're having the party."

"Of course. I'm on my way back."

Ford was trying to act like it was no big, but Ryan was worried.

"Phil? Phil, man. I need you."

Phil left the man he was talking to immediately. "Sure. What's wrong?"

"Bleu went out snowmobiling this morning, and they're not back. More than an hour late. I need to get back to the ranch."

"Let's go." Phil took his arm and just marched his butt back to the fancy-assed Jeep Phil drove, no question. They hopped in and moved out of the VIP lot slowly, but once they were on the main highway, they were booking.

"Ford says they're expecting a storm. I—what if he's hurt?"

"We'll find them. There's a ranch full of cowboys and pro skiers. We'll find them."

"Right. Right." He would get out on the cross-country skis if he had to.

"Relax. I bet they broke down and are trudging through the snow singing Willie Nelson songs."

"Ha-ha." Did Bleu even know any Willie songs? His dad played the guitar, so he probably did.

"Yeah, I'm trying to help."

"I know, hon. I do. I'm just freaked-out. If Bleu is hurt or lost…. Floyd isn't with him."

"Can Floyd find him? Does that really work? Like with sniffing and stuff?"

"Maybe." He hadn't thought of that. He texted Ford, *Can anyone take Floyd? He might be able to help.*

I'll see, came back.

He tapped his fingers on his phone. Okay. Okay, how far would Stoney have taken Bleu? Surely the wranglers knew the route. They took people out all the time. The suits they used for snowmobiling had avalanche beacons. They could do this.

The drive seemed to take forever, and even more ominous, there was no word from Ford.

The ranch looked like an ant's nest that had been disturbed, people running around like idiots. There was still a big party going on, and now they had a major storm to prepare for.

Ryan leaped out of the Jeep and ran for the main house. He needed to find Ford.

Who he found was Quartz.

Fuck.

"Daddy wasn't with you, then." The words weren't a question.

"No, kiddo. Where's your Uncle Ford?" He didn't want to make Quartz scared.

"In the office."

"Thank you." He pressed a hand to Quartz's shoulder before going to find Ford. He knocked, but he wasn't going to be put off.

"Come in." Ford's face was a thundercloud, the little Bluetooth earpiece blinking. "Hey. Hold up. Can you get me a helicopter out here? Goddammit! I know there's a storm, but my husband is out there with a guest that's blind. It's a big fucking deal."

He waited, wincing when he realized that had to be search and rescue.

"Fine. Tomorrow. Fuck you too." Ford slammed down the phone. "They haven't been gone long enough, and that storm is coming in. I'll see if Noah Wright can help. His husband is doing the party for us."

"What about the avalanche beacons?"

"Nothing. Someone has to be close enough for it to get the signal. Stoney would have called in if it was just run-of-the-mill. He took a radio."

"Dammit. Dammit. What can I do? What do I need to do?"

"Stay here for a few? Man the radio. I have to find Noah and let the crew know what's happening."

"Okay. Sure. Quartz is freaking out a little, just FYI."

"Can he come sit with you? Floyd went out with Doogie."

"Sure. Sure, of course." What the hell was he supposed to do with a kid who had a lost father?

"He won't bug you, I swear, but it will be good for him to have company. Geoff and Tiny are so—"

"Go. Just go find someone who can help, huh?"

"Yeah." Ford headed off at a run, leaving him there alone.

Christ. He checked his phone, hoping Bleu was going to call or text.

"Come on, babe. Let me know you're okay…."

Bleu had to be okay. They were just getting back together. Ryan couldn't lose him now.

Chapter Sixteen

BLEU woke up confused and cold, the smells of snow and fuel everywhere. *Okay. Okay, focus. First, think before you panic.* He reached up and touched his face. *Gloves. Helmet. Goggles. So, outside.*

"Hello? Hello, can anyone hear me?" Lord, his voice sounded loud in his ears.

No answer came, and he started to panic, because he couldn't—

Just as that thought started, reality popped back into his head.

Snowmobiling. With Stoney.

"Stoney? Stoney, can you hear me?"

When there was no answer, he absolutely panicked for a moment, sure he was dead and he just didn't know it.

Then he took a deep breath of cold air.

Okay, start searching. He reached out as far as he could in all directions. He didn't find anything, so he scooted over to sit in the line he'd drawn and repeated the motions, calling for Stoney again and again.

He vaguely remembered falling backward, downhill, so that was where he moved. Down, then doing his feeling around.

Down. Feel. Down. Feel. Do—

The snowmobile. He felt carefully, finding it upside down, the ski-deals up in the air. "Okay, so you fell off. Where did you go?"

He moved around the sled, stopping short when he ran into something—someone—sticking out. "Fuck."

Snow boots. Right. If they were perpendicular, then maybe so was Stoney's head. He moved back uphill, then worked around the sled to feel on the other side. *Okay, head. Right. Fuck.*

"Stoney? Can you hear me?" He would really like Stoney to talk so he could figure out how hurt he was, how to fix this and not feel so alone.

He pushed a little, trying to decide whether to move the sled or dig Stoney out. He pulled off his gloves, searching for Stoney's eyes. Closed, but they were moving under the closed lids.

Thank God. Pulling the gloves back on, he sat and thought a moment. Stoney had an emergency kit on the snowmobile.

First thing, get Stoney from under the snowmobile. Then get him warmed up. Third, find out if the beacon deal Stoney had told him about was working.

"Right. I have a plan."

He moved to the front of the snowmobile because he'd felt the skis had handles.

Stoney had said if they flipped, the seat and handlebars would act like a fulcrum, so he was supposed to flip it from the skis. He could do this. Bleu just wasn't sure if he could do it without hurting Stoney.

"Please, God. Please. I'm going to be the ultimate in calm and not idiot, and you're going to help me help him. Deal? Deal. Rock on. Amen." He lifted and shoved as hard as he could, twisting and stumbling through the snow as he fought to get the sled off Stoney.

His feet slid, and he grunted, grinding his teeth to stay upright. Bleu shouted like a weight lifter or a martial artist, and the snowmobile went over so fast that he staggered off to one side so he didn't fall on Stoney.

"Okay. Okay." He collapsed next to Stoney, panting hard. "Let's make sure I didn't break you."

Bleu pulled off his gloves again, this time feeling Stoney's pulse. A little jumpy, but not weak. Now he would… what? Check for injuries? Yes. Oh Lord, there was blood on Stoney's head….

Suddenly he could hear Ryan in his head. His lover had given him instructions more than once back in Boulder, just in case he found himself alone and/or injured in the snow, because once you wandered off a trail, you could get lost fast.

"Stay warm," he said along with his mental Ryan. "That's the biggest thing. Don't exert yourself enough to sweat. Too late for that. All right. So warmth is most important, bud."

He went to the snowmobile and started searching. *Emergency kit. Emergency kit.*

Ha! There was a pack behind the seat, and it was still intact. Yay. Right. He struggled to get it loose, then opened it. There was what he thought was juice or water packets, packets of food, what he imagined was a first aid kit.

Bingo. Survival blankets. They caught sun on the outside, and had a slick, reflective surface inside to use their own body heat. Ryan had explained them to him on one of their long ago camping trips to the mountains.

He laid one out and rolled Stoney up onto it, trying to brush the snow off Stoney as he did. The suits they wore protected them some, but Stoney was on the ground, and had been for who knew how long. Bleu checked to make sure Stoney was faceup, then covered him with another blanket.

"Okay. Good. Now, I have to find the beacon deal. Is it like a radio…. Oh. You have a radio. I heard it. I heard it crackle."

He pulled off his gloves and started searching for something like a walkie-talkie.

If he could just get a hold of the ranch, well, he could get them saved.

Stoney needed saving.

Chapter Seventeen

“NOAH’S going to see what he can do….”

Someone Ryan didn’t know came pushing into the office.

“You’re not Ford.”

“No, Mason, this is Mr. Ryan. Mr. Bleu is his friend.” He’d almost forgotten Quartz was there, if he was honest, until the kid piped up.

“Hey. Ford is out scaring up more searchers.” Ryan stood, holding out a hand. “I’m manning the radio.”

“Oh, excellent. I’m Mason. My husband is trying to find a helicopter that can get here before the storm.”

“Thank you both so much for your help.” He was an athlete. He wanted to be out there helping, but he didn’t know the terrain as well as Stoney and Ford’s people, and he would just be in the way.

"Anything for them. Anything." Mason went to Quartz. "You okay?"

"When am I going to be big enough to go help?"

"Soon, kiddo. You're big enough to help me right now, if you want." Mason met Ryan's gaze over Quartz's head, his expression telling Ryan he was being kind. "Geoff and Tiny have to help with the party, but we need sandwiches and coffee for the guys who are out searching. Are you game?"

"Yeah. Yeah, I can do that. Do you want one, Mr. Ryan?"

"I would love that, thank you." He'd planned to gorge himself with Bleu after the event, so he was actually feeling a bit light-headed.

"I'll be right back, then," Quartz said, leaving with Mason.

"Jesus, Bleu. Where are you?" He dropped his head in his hands, feeling utterly useless. He hated this. Hated it. Bleu was perfectly capable, he knew that, but he was up against a lot with this storm.

"Hello? Hello, I need help. Is someone out there?" The radio crackled to life.

Ryan snatched up the handset. "Bleu?"

"Ryan? Ryan, can you hear me? There was an accident. Stoney's out cold and bleeding. I have him in the emergency blanket, but I need medical assistance."

"Okay. The wranglers and some of the guests who have search-and-rescue training are out looking for you. Do you have any idea where you are?"

"There was a hill. We went down and tried to go back up."

"A hill. Describe exactly what you felt." Quartz walked in with a plate, and Ryan waved at him frantically. "Get your uncle," he mouthed.

Quartz nodded and ran.

"There was a big hill, all the way down, then we went around and around, but on the way up, something happened. Stoney was under the sled. I got him out. There's snow everywhere. Soft snow. Deep."

"I hear you. Sounds like you're in a valley of some sort. A depression. Do you have an emergency kit?"

"Yes. I got the blankets out and covered Stoney. What does the beacon thing feel like?"

"If you went downhill that fast, it will be activated." The beacons always activated at fast downward motion. "It should be in your suit. Or around Stoney's neck. It will be like, uh, a small flip-phone shape. Or like your dad's glucometer."

"Okay. Okay, I'm going to hunt for it. I need both hands. I'll be back."

He wanted to shout for Bleu not to go, but they needed to get found before that storm got bad. A glance out the window told him it was already snowing.

Ford burst in. "Where are they?"

"Bleu says they zoomed down a huge hill into a bowl of some sort. They did some laps before starting up the other side, but that's where they flipped."

"Doesn't Stoney know where they are, for fuck's sake?"

"He's out cold, Ford. Bleu has him in survival blankets, and he's making sure the beacons are on. Tanner has a transponder, right?"

Ford slammed his hand against the desk, making him jump. Then he calmed, like someone had pulled a curtain down over his frustration. "Yeah, and he and Doogie have both run guide trips with Stoney. They might know where this bowl is. I'll get Tanner on his cell to keep the radio free if I can."

He nodded, eyes on the receiver.

"You got this. I'm going to call Tanner and get medical up here."

"Okay. I'll holler at you when Stoney wakes up." That just seemed like the right thing to say.

"You do that." With that Ford was gone, and he sat, waiting for Bleu to come back.

He grabbed the sandwich Quartz had brought him, because eating his feelings was more productive than screaming.

"Hey, I found Stoney's beacon. It's beeping." Bleu sounded out of breath.

"Good. That's good. Okay, so, next we need to get you and Stoney both warmer while you wait."

"Should I go find wood? I found the matches and put them in my pocket."

"It may come to that, babe, but most of the wood will be wet and will take forever to catch. There should be hand warmers in the emergency kit. Do you remember what they feel like? Little square plastic things that heat up when you hold them?"

"I know. I have some in my boots from when we started. Do I put them on Stoney's chest, do you think?"

"Put them in his gloves and boots. Put more in yours too. You'll have to huddle up with him to share whatever heat you can. Your kit will also have glow sticks instead of flares. They're super bright, and all you have to do is crack them like the ones at Halloween. When the guys get near, they'll see them." He just kept talking, thinking of anything that would help.

"Okay. Okay. I'm going to do that and see if I can't wrap Stoney's head up. His heart rate is strong, stable."

"Okay. Try to get his head up off the ground too. That will help." He could tell Bleu was doing, not talking, when no answer came. *God, please let them find Bleu and Stoney soon. Please.*

BLEU was scared to death, but he tried to keep it at bay. People knew they were missing now, knew Stoney was hurt. They would come for them. He just had to keep them warm and keep Stoney alive.

No big deal.

Except it was snowing hard, and the only cover they had was the snowmobile.

"I'm so sorry, man. I didn't know there'd be an accident." He held Stoney's head in his lap, cradling it.

The air was colder, so it had to be getting darker, with the storm, he guessed. He'd put out three light thingies, and at Ryan's command, he'd had a pouch of water and a small bag of peanuts. The radio wasn't off, but he wasn't using it to babble because he had to conserve the batteries. He knew there were flashlight batteries in the emergency kit, but who knew if they were the same as the ones in the radio? Bleu doubted it.

Ryan checked with him every twenty minutes, and every twenty minutes he said he was fine, and every twenty minutes he was lying. He was scared to death.

"Bleu?" Stoney's voice was rough as a cob and barely there. "It's cold."

"Oh. Oh, hey there. It totally is. You whacked your head but good. You… you want water?" He grabbed the radio. "Ryan? Ryan, he's awake."

"Thank God. I'll tell Ford."

Bleu nodded and moved just enough to grab the pack. He didn't want to dump Stoney on the ground.

"Water is a great idea. My head is killing me."

“Yeah, it sucked big-time. Do you think you can sit up, or would that be bad?”

Stoney lifted his head a fraction of an inch, then gagged. “Bad. Definitely bad. I can wiggle my toes, though.”

Relief flooded him.

“That’s good. Really good. I’ll get you the water.”

“Are you okay? Did you hit your head?”

He was fine, barring a little bit of a sore ankle. “I have to admit, Stoney. I-I can’t see.”

Stoney stiffened, then chuffed out a laugh. “You fuck.”

Bleu laughed a little. “I think my head is fine. I’m sure I have bruises, but you were bleeding hard.”

“It don’t feel cracked, but I bet I’m concussed some.”

“Do you know where we are? Do you know how to tell them?”

“We were in the bowl, right? Did you tell them that?”

“Uh-huh. I think so. I told them we went down and then went around and around and….”

A loud barking filled the air, shocking him.

“Floyd!”

“Careful!” Stoney said, and Bleu remembered he had Stoney on his lap.

“Sorry. Sorry. Floyd! Help!”

A few moments later, Floyd came bounding down the rise at them, and the low hum of an engine came after him. The engine stopped on top of the hill. “Boss? Bleu?” Doogie shouted down.

“We’re here! We’re down here!” He grabbed Floyd, trying not to cry, because he’d done good so far. His boy was pretty warm, really, for all that he had snow on his fur.

Floyd barked and licked his face, clearly overjoyed.

"Hang on, fellers!" He could hear Doogie talking on either a radio or cell. Maybe a cell, because his radio….

He snatched it up. "Ryan! Doogie is here!"

Chapter Eighteen

"RYAN! Doogie is here!"

Ryan's knees buckled, and he sat hard. "Oh, thank God."

Then he sprang back up and ran, searching for Ford. "They found them!"

Ford looked at him, utterly disbelieving for a moment. Then color flooded his cheeks. "Oh God."

"Doogie. He's in the small snowcat, right?"

"Right." Ford frantically dialed his phone. "Tanner? Doogie has them. He has the coordinates. Yes. I'm trying, but we don't have a chopper. Okay."

Ford hung up. "There's no way the cat can get down in a bowl, but Tanner says he's not far, and he can get them up the slope with ropes and a travois once he gets there."

"Should I go? Can I help? What can I do?"

"You can help get Bleu's cabin ready for him. Medical will set up here, but as long as he's not badly hurt, he'll just need to be warm and comfortable and hydrated." Ford brooked no argument. "Then we wait together."

Mason, the party planner, and his huge Texan husband, Noah, walked up. "We've got the party handled. We'll do the unveiling and all the ta-das, while you two deal with your men. I'm sorry about the chopper, but I'm lighting a fire under search and rescue. This can't happen again."

"Thank you." Ford shook hands with both of them. "I'm just—they're on their way home soon."

"Of course. We can handle the business." Mason and Noah disappeared as fast as they came.

"I'm going to get hot tea and soup from the kitchen." He started thinking about what Bleu would need. Warm towels. A bath. Maybe some whiskey.

"Go for it. Keep your phone handy."

"I will." He hustled, knowing it would take time to get Stoney and Bleu back, but needing to be busy. He detoured to find Dan and Phil in the great room, almost having forgotten them. "They're on their way home."

"Good." Dan stood up, came right to him. "What can I do?"

"Can you see if you can get someone to change the sheets in his room and get some extra blankets? He's going to need rest and warmth." He knew Dan was frantic, and he understood needing to move.

"I can do that."

"You'll need to be Bleu's mouthpiece at the party for the unveiling too. Please."

"Of course."

"Phil, can you pinch-hit for me? I know Mike was going to be looking for me."

"Of course I can. If there's anything else I can do at all…."

"You've been a huge help keeping me sane," Dan said. "We'll join forces at the party?"

"Of course. I'll go get dressed and meet you there." Phil waited for Dan to go before searching Ryan's eyes. "You're okay?"

"I will be. Stoney hit his head, but Bleu is fine, if bruised and cold. They're rescued, so I just have to wait." He gave Phil a hug. "Thank you so much for everything today."

"Of course. You know I'm your friend before anything else. Even before the work."

He'd known, but this time Phil had proven it.

"I appreciate it so much." He squeezed one more time. "Okay, off to the kitchen."

Tiny and Geoff were working their asses off, and he hated to bother, but it was for Bleu, so he'd interrupt. "I need to know where I can get soup for Bleu. I'll do the work, just tell me where."

"There's a thermos of chicken soup. A thermos of hot sweet tea. Here's a bottle of brandy. Once they've been home a few hours, I'll send cocoa."

Tears actually stung his eyes. "You're like Santa Claus."

"Or a really smart Saint Bernard." Geoff winked. "Have you eaten?"

"Quartz brought me a sandwich."

"Well, take a piece of pizza with you too."

"Thanks, guys. Can I take anything to Ford?"

"Quartz is on duty," Tiny said. "Go on now."

He went, because he had all he could carry and then some.

Dan had the sheets changed, a bunch of quilts on the beds, and the towel warmer going. Then he pushed Ryan into a chair and fed him pizza and a beer.

The pizza filled his belly, and the beer relaxed him enough to just sit a minute.

"I have to go hit the party," Dan said. "There's a lot of people to prep for Bleu not being there. You okay?"

"I will be once he's in my arms." That was the God's honest truth.

"Text me when he gets in? I just—"

"I get it." He smiled at Dan, grateful that he was Bleu's friend.

"Thanks. I'm going to get on my monkey suit and be the fancy Santa Fe gallery owner."

"Gotcha." He waved, then moved back to Bleu's bedroom. He found warm pajamas and a chew bone for Floyd.

Then he settled in to wait.

They were found.

Chapter Nineteen

"I'M going to need your help, Bleu." Doogie's voice was rough as a cob, the smoking catching up to him in this frigid situation.

"Sure. I can do whatever."

"We're going to have to build a travois to get Stoney up the hill."

"I c'n walk," Stoney muttered.

"Shut up, boss."

A travois? What the fuck? "Sure, Doogie. I can help. Just point me and shoot me."

"Good man. I tried the sled, and it won't start. Might have a fuel leak. So basically a travois is a fancy word for two long poles tied with a knot at one end and a piece of hide stretched between them. We got these blankets, and I got some long branches. I'll rig a piece of blanket under Stoney's arms to hold him on, but I need you to help assemble." That was more words than he'd ever heard Doogie utter at one time.

"Like this?" He drew a shape in the snow, a vee with an indention in the middle to represent the blanket.

"That's it exactly." Doogie chuckled. "Look at us, all speaking the same language. I need to go get more rope out of the cat."

"Okay. I'll get the blanket fastened."

"I can fucking walk up the goddamn hill!" He'd never seen Stoney so mad, so out of control. Too bad he couldn't even sit up without puking.

"Hey, can you get on the radio and talk to Quartz? Ry says he's a little stressed out."

"Shit. Yeah, of course." Stoney fumbled for the radio, hand shaking madly. "Ford? Can I talk to Quartz?"

That gave Stoney something to do while Bleu tried to be a functional adult and make a travois. Did they give badges for this? They should. Functioning blind in emergency situations. Creating tools that heretofore he'd never fucking imagined. Not having a screaming meltdown in the snow.

"View hallooo!" A rush of snow came down the hill, and along with it came what he thought was Tanner, landing next to him. "Hey, good job, Bleu. Doogie is gonna stay up there and coordinate ropes."

"Thanks. Uh, he's a little touchy."

"Y'think? Hey, boss, you ready to let me haul your skinny ass up the hill?"

"Fuck off."

"Excellent." Tanner grunted, and Stoney groaned and panted, so he thought Tanner must be rigging the thing under his arms like Doogie had said.

Bleu started putting things into the emergency kit. "Will we leave the snowmobile here or bring it back with us?"

"We'll leave it for now. I'll come back with the cat and winch it out later." Tanner was just really pleased to be there, he thought. "This storm is a bitch. It's because we have the big party, you know. It's like a thing. We hold a shindig, the entire fucking world loses its collective mind. The ski resorts ought to pay us to hold parties."

"Tanner…." Stoney's voice was almost gone.

"I got you, boss. Okay, Doogie! Slow and sure! Bleu, I will be back for you. Stay put."

The winch wasn't whirring, so he thought they were using Tanner's horse to pull Stoney up.

Floyd stayed with him, solid and sure. He thought maybe Floyd would be with him for the next month, solid. "Hey, boy. Let's get this shit in the bag before the snow gets any deeper."

It sure felt like it was unstoppable, like no matter how much he brushed off his face and head, there was still more.

He finished packing the stuff they could still use in the emergency pack, then slung it on his back. Floyd wasn't wearing his harness, so he waited until Tanner slid down to join him.

"Okay, buddy. The rope is down. The easiest way up is to walk and pull ourselves up holding it. How are your feet?"

"Cold, but I'm okay." The ankle would hold fine, at least until he got his boot loose. Then all bets were off. "Let's do this. I need to get Floyd warmed up."

"I hear you. Doogie says he's a trouper. Like he knew he was looking for you." Tanner helped him get ahold of the rope. His gloves had enough grip that he left them on. Tanner came up behind him, shoulder kinda in his butt.

It was harder than he'd imagined it would be. He was frozen and exhausted, and his stores were spent from fear and stress. Still, he made himself pull his knees out of the snow, over and over.

He was shaking and breathing so hard, he was light-headed by the time the ground leveled out. That surprised him so much that he staggered and went to his knees. Floyd yelped and came right to him to lick his face.

"Good man," Tanner told him. "Let's get you in the cat."

"Okay." He couldn't move. Not another inch. Not even for the promise of being out of the snow.

Tanner lifted him up with surprising strength for such a pocket cowboy, and Doogie was right there too, helping him into the vehicle. The warmth was shocking, and he felt as if his heart damn near stopped.

His tears were frozen on his cheeks, which was funny, because he didn't remember crying, not even once.

"It's okay, man. You did good. You just breathe for a minute. I can't give you a blanket yet. We have to warm you up in stages or too much blood will rush back to your heart and boom. I have a towel. Let me clean the snow out of Floyd's paws real quick." Tanner still sounded ridiculously happy.

"You need anything, Tan?" Doogie asked.

"How much tea do you have? I could use some."

"I got enough to give you another thermos. You want to ride or drive?"

"As if I would let you ride Mollie back in this mess, you crazy old man."

Bleu stopped listening to the negotiations. Instead he curled around Floyd and held on, both man and beast shaking like they'd taken earthquake pills.

"I'm coming home, son," Stoney said. "You hold on. I'm on my way."

He nodded against Floyd's ruff. Right. They were on their way.

Chapter Twenty

IT seemed like hours before Ryan heard the hum of the little snowcat's engine. Maybe it was.

He heard it, though, and he hopped up from the chair he'd been dozing in and ran out into the yard in front of the main house.

The party was in full swing, sleighs running people up and down, music ringing out, but for him, Quartz, and Ford, the only thing that mattered was the headlights buzzing toward the main house.

Ford clapped him on the back, grinning this crazy smile, as if his face was completely out of his control. "They're here."

"They are. Into your living room?"

"Yeah. The medics are waiting."

"Good deal."

Doogie pulled up and killed the engine, and Ford ran up, gathered Stoney in his arms, and ran with Quartz to the house. Bleu stood there, covered in blood, a vicious bruise swelling one eye closed, pale as milk.

"Ryan?"

"Right here, babe." He strode over to take Bleu in his arms. "Let's get you and Floyd inside, huh?" He wrapped an arm around Bleu's waist to support him and hustle him into the house.

Bleu stumbled forward, but he walked, so Ryan let him. Hell, he wasn't sure if he could carry Bleu if he had to.

The house was warm and bright, and the medics whisked Bleu away from him almost too fast. He stayed close, wanting Bleu to know he was there, but he also knew Floyd needed attention, so he got a towel and dried the big shepherd off, then wrapped him in a blanket.

"Floyd—"

"I got him, babe. He's gonna be fine." Water and a snack next. For the dog.

Floyd honestly didn't seem worse for wear. He kept his eyes on Bleu and whined to get closer.

"I know, buddy. Soon."

The EMTs barked out things like blood pressure and oxygen levels. There was no sign of frostbite on either man, which was a blessing, though Stoney was prehypothermic.

"I'd like to take him down to Aspen, just to have a CAT scan on his head."

"No way," Stoney snarled. "I'm fine."

"Baby, we need to make sure."

"If I still feel bad tomorrow, we'll go." Stubbornness colored Stoney's voice.

"You were out a long time," Ford countered.

"Tomorrow. We have the party."

"Fuck the party!" Ford's veins were popping out in his neck.

"Uncle Ford!" Quartz was scandalized.

"If you start vomiting, have any slurring of speech or motor control issues, you need to go down to the ER, okay?" The EMT seemed unfazed.

"Mr. Bridey, are you having any pain in your head?" Bleu's medic was probing the area around that poor eye.

"Well, that don't feel great, but no. I'm just tired and cold."

"You have some pretty amazing contusions, but I don't think you injured the eye socket. I think you need rest and fluids, but if you have any headaches or dizziness, head down with Mr. River tomorrow to the hospital, okay?"

"Fair enough. Can I go? Please? I need a shower."

"Lukewarm at best. Are you staying with him?"

Ryan nodded firmly. "I am. What do I need to do?"

"Just keep an eye on him. Lukewarm shower, fluids, make sure he eats a light meal in the next few hours."

"I got it." Ryan unbent enough to smile. "Thank you."

"Glad we could help."

Ryan rose, going to Ford for a moment. "If you need any help…."

"Your man saved Stoney's life. I'm grateful." Ford nodded at Bleu. "Go on and get him settled."

He didn't need to be told again. Bleu's one foot was all bandaged, and they'd told him not to put weight on it. "You want to do a three-legged race, babe, or try Ice Capades in the wheelchair they brought?"

"No wheelchairs. I want to go now." Poor Bleu was at the end of his thread, tremors rocking him constantly.

There was a storm coming, and Ryan knew his lover didn't want that to be a public display.

"Come on, then." He helped Bleu bundle up in a huge coat that belonged to Tiny, and half carried, half dragged him to the cabin. Someone was digging out crutches, he thought, and would deliver them later.

The fire was going already, and he didn't even ask. He just bundled Bleu into the bathroom and started stripping his lover down as the water warmed.

Bleu shook, clinging to his shoulders.

Ryan undressed too, then stepped into the shower with Bleu, helping to hold him up. Tomorrow there would be hot tubbing if Bleu felt up to it. He had wraps to redo Bleu's ankle, and God knew Ryan was used to foot injuries.

"I'm sorry," Bleu whispered. "I missed the party."

"You did. So did Stoney." Ryan chuckled. "He's kinda peeved at the world."

"Yeah. He's angry." Bleu took one shaky breath after another. "It all happened really fast."

"I bet. Snow and ice can be vicious." He washed the grime off, letting Bleu lean on him for balance. "You did good, though. You didn't panic."

He couldn't begin to imagine opening his eyes and not seeing anything. Much less being blind and lost with no way to wake up the person you were with. He would have lost his shit.

Bleu had held it together like it was nothing.

"I did panic, but only inside." Bleu laughed, then hiccupped out a tiny sob.

"You did so good, babe. You did. And you're here and safe, all of you." Ryan stroked Bleu's back, holding him up with the other arm. He would let Bleu get it out.

Bleu hid his face in the curve of Ryan's shoulder and shook, and if there were tears, well, they got washed away by the spray of the shower, so no one would ever know. No one.

By the time the storm inside was over, Ryan turned off the water to dry Bleu with the warm towels. Then he took Bleu to bed and wrapped his ankle in dry wraps, bundling him up with blankets and, yeah, Floyd.

"I'm going to bring you some tea, and you'll need to drink it. The cold takes it out of you."

"You're staying?" Bleu reached for him, holding on to his wrist. "Please?"

"I am. The thermos is in the main room, is all." Ryan brought Bleu's hand to his mouth to kiss it.

"Oh. Sorry. Right. I just… I don't want to be alone right now."

"I know. I got you." Ryan grinned. "Two minutes."

"Right. Two minutes."

"Stay awake."

"I will."

"I'm serious…," Ryan warned.

To his pleasure, Bleu started laughing for him, the sound a little thready but real and honest.

"Be right back." The tea had sat in the thermos long enough to be less than piping hot, so he popped it in the microwave. He did the same with the chicken soup.

Then he headed back to make sure Bleu was awake, though really, he'd managed to stay awake in the freezing cold for hours, so the head injury was minor.

Mostly he just wanted Bleu awake and talking to him, proving that everything was okay.

"Hey. Tea. Unless you want the chicken broth."

"Tea first." Bleu sounded like he'd been on a three-day bender.

"Right on, babe." He put the mug in Bleu's fingers, but they were shaking too hard to hold on. Poor baby. "Here, don't get mad." He held the cup to Bleu's lips.

Bleu held his wrists and drank deep, almost gulping the tea down.

"Hey, easy. There's more, I swear." He knew how it felt, though. After a long day on the slopes, he was dying of thirst, so Bleu had to be crazy with it. "I got you."

"God, I'm dry. Like July in Santa Fe dry."

"Yeah, it will wear you out and freezer burn you." He poured another cup of tea from the stuff he'd warmed up and poured back in the thermos. "Have a little more, but don't make yourself sick."

"Right. It's really good. Do you need some?"

"I'm good. I'll probably see if they'll bring us some real food in a few hours…."

Bleu leaned back, both eyes closed now. "How was your exhibition?"

"Good. I shredded it." He reached up to stroke Bleu's hair, the heavy strands tangling around his fingers. "I'm sorry you missed the big unveiling."

"So did Stoney, and Ford had it commissioned for him."

"I know." Shit happened. That was the one constant in life, wasn't it?

Bleu shuddered, rocking himself. "I don't think I did anything wrong…."

"Tanner said the sled hit a fallen tree. That's an act of God, babe."

"Oh. It was hidden under the snow."

"Exactly. That's why they call snowmobiling an extreme sport." He grinned. "You just happened not to be on a flat, which made for ack. That's a technical term, you know."

"Yeah? Ack is right. I woke up, and… well, it sucked."

Sucked. Yeah, yeah, Mr. Understatement, he guessed so.

He grinned, shaking his head. That was his Bleu. "You did fab."

"Yeah. We all made it. That has to be enough, right?"

"It is. I mean, Stoney would have died without you, babe." He thought it was important to note that.

"He wouldn't have been out there without me."

"Bah. You know that man loves to snowmobile. He goes out constantly. Don't believe for a second that you were at fault. It was an accident, pure and simple."

"I just—someone else would have been able to do more."

"What?" Ryan poked Bleu's arm gently. "Tanner said the sled was a goner. You kept Stoney as warm as you could, found the radio to tell us where you were, used the light sticks to mark your position, and got home in one piece. You did as much as anyone could in that situation, sighted or not."

"I didn't panic. God, I wanted to. I wanted to scream, but I was afraid if I started, I wouldn't be able to stop." Bleu leaned into him, skin still too damned cold. "It's silly, but it's true."

"It's human nature." He set the thermos aside so he could crawl into bed with Bleu. He'd forgotten to put clothes on, and it was chilly.

"Oh." Bleu snuggled right in, tangling their legs together. "Oh, love. Stay."

"I will." He wasn't going anywhere for at least a few hours. Maybe all night.

He kissed the top of Bleu's head, and he had almost dozed off when he heard Bleu's words.

Love.

Yes. Love. Stay. These were the important things. They had a shit load to talk about, but right now, that was enough.

Chapter Twenty-One

BLEU had never been so sore in his whole life. Never. Not even when he'd misjudged the steps in front of the library and gone down an entire flight of concrete.

"Oh God. Kill me now," he muttered, trying his damnedest to remember where the bathroom was.

"Hey, hon. The door is to your left." Dan sounded subdued, but he wasn't making a big deal, which was nice.

"Thank you. Sorry. Yesterday was… rough."

"Y'think?" Dan's voice was dry as dust.

"Fuck off." He chuckled, though, because it was true. Yesterday had been… endless. Ryan had been proud, though, and that meant a shit-ton to him. "I need a hot shower."

"I'll come sit with you, make sure you don't fall." As he opened his mouth to argue, Dan said, "It's not like I haven't seen it all, and your ankle is huge."

"Right. Just no ogling."

"I don't find bruises sexy. I prefer my sex symbols in tuxedos and shiny shoes. Bond style."

"You are a fucking weirdo, man."

"I am. Come on." Dan took him to the bathroom and even got the water going.

He stripped down and stepped into the spray, the heat immediately helping the sore muscles, his swollen screaming joints. His foot hurt, but even it was so much better for a night's rest. He thought Ryan was gone, but then so was Floyd, so maybe Ryan had just taken Floyd out to pee.

"You know that you could have died out there. Was it worth it?" Dan asked quietly.

"I could have died here. I could die right now. It was fun, until the accident. It was like flying."

"So you're saying you'd go again? Really?"

"Probably not today. I'm sore. But again? Yeah. Yeah, I'd try again."

"Ryan says I should stop trying to make you less than you are." Dan laughed, the sound a little torn. "You know it's just worry, right? I do this to everyone."

"You're a good man. You always have been. A bit of a dork, but a good man."

"Thanks." Dan chuckled, this time with more humor. "I was scared to death, but Ryan was a champ. He was amazing."

"He is. I love him." He rinsed the shampoo out of his hair so he didn't have to worry about Dan's response.

"Are you listening to me?" Dan asked when he was back out of the rushing water.

"Nope. Not that I ever do."

"Asshat." Dan said it fondly. "Your towel is in the warmer."

"Thank you. How was the party? Have I asked that already?"

"Nope. It was amazing. The response to your piece was stunning. I can't wait for Stoney to see it."

"Me either." He smiled at that thought. "Have we heard whether he's okay? Does Ryan have Floyd?"

"I assume Ryan has Floyd, yes. I'm not sure. Stoney is okay, though Ford is making him go to the hospital today."

"That sucks, but it's probably for the best. Is it still snowing?"

"Nope. It cleared off about five this morning and is viciously cold out there. I was—do you think we could stay on another day, at least? I'd like the roads to get cleared some."

"That's fine with me. I'm not ready to move on yet." He wasn't ready to leave Ryan, although who knew? Maybe Ryan left today.

"Oh, good." Dan's relief was so palpable, Bleu felt bad. "Here. Towel."

"Mmm, warm."

"Indeed. That's the nice thing about towel warmers."

"Shut up, turd bucket."

He heard Dan's snort, and didn't that make him cackle?

"Hello?" Ryan's voice came from the main room. "Dan? Bleu?"

"In the bathroom, man," Dan called out. "I was worried he'd slip."

"Is everyone naked?" Ryan was laughing, and Floyd burst through the partly open door, his nails clicking on the tile.

"Only Bleu, and he has a towel."

"You mean you're not naked, Dan?" He put all his sarcasm into the words.

"No. I am not." Dan sounded so prim.

"Well, come on, naked and not. I brought breakfast. Geoff sent enough for all of us. For a week."

"Yeah? Cool. I'm starving. Is there bacon?" His nose was stuffed up. He fucking hated that.

"Bacon, sausage, and ham. Eggs and waffles. Cinnamon rolls. Hot syrup and butter." Ryan was just as cheerful as, well, Tanner had been yesterday.

"Waffles…." He stepped out of the tub and into Ryan's arms. "Oh, hello."

"Hey. Dan traded me. He's out there arranging breakfast into beauty, I have no doubt."

"Uh-huh. Kiss me." He knew they couldn't linger, but he wanted a kiss. Maybe he needed one.

Ryan held him up easily, letting him wrap his arms around Ryan's neck. The kiss was slow but deep, really exploring him completely. Bleu let himself melt, let Ryan hold him and keep him warm as they moaned together.

"Ahem." That wasn't Dan. "Come on, horndogs. Breakfast."

"Phil, who let you in?"

Phil was clearly not where he could see anything or Ryan probably wouldn't sound amused.

"Dan the man. We're having breakfast together. You should get less wet."

"Go to the other room, Phil. My wetness is not for your edification." Bleu didn't snap, but he did say it firmly.

"True fact," Ryan agreed. "Scram."

Phil stomped away, and Ryan helped dry him off. "Clean jammies or sweats?"

"Sweats. Are you leaving today, Ry?" *Can you stay? Will you stay?*

"No, I can stay as long as I need to." Ryan rubbed his arms. "Come on, babe. Clothes first."

"Right. Clothes. Breakfast." Then the hard part. Maybe the good part. Wasn't it time for the good part by now? He wanted their fairy-tale ending.

Ryan helped him dress. "Do you want the crutches?"

"God no. I would kill Floyd or something."

They both laughed, but his ankle wasn't as bad as all that—tender and swollen, yes, but not as bad as when he'd hurt it playing baseball in school.

"Okay, breakfast ho!" Ryan felt so good, arm around him, hip pressed to his.

The whole main room of the cabin smelled like heaven. Syrup and pastry, bacon and sausage.

He sat, taking the coffee mug Dan offered him with thanks.

"Mmm. God, I could just get super fat here," Phil said.

"I think the people who work here work so hard they need the calories." Bleu shrugged. He wasn't concerned. He ate when he was hungry and when the food smelled good.

"Yeah." Ryan's voice was a little strained. "I used to be that way when I was working out eight hours a day."

"And now you can breathe, love. You're an artist now, not a competitive athlete." He leaned into Ryan, cuddling close. "Share waffles with me?"

"Yes. That sounds perfect. Do you still like lots of butter and a little syrup?"

"You remember."

"Butter is…," Phil started, and Bleu held a hand up.

"Proof there is a God and He loves us. Don't harsh my mellow, man. This is breakfast."

Dan chuckled. "Bleu is passionate about his breakfast."

"I am." He nodded happily. "I love it all. Well, except smoked salmon. No way is fish acceptable for breakfast."

Ryan snorted. "Unless it's trout caught and cooked right out of the river."

"That's a camping thing," Bleu pointed out. "I haven't gone camping since… well, you."

"We'll have to go." Ryan said it so easily, which gave Bleu hope. There would be an after this. A soft bit of bread touched his lips, so he opened up his mouth to take in a bite of waffles.

"Mmm…," Bleu hummed, the mixture just perfect.

"Jesus, does he know he looks like he's being fucked when he eats?"

Ryan cleared his throat. "Inappropriate, Phillip."

"Do I? Really?"

Dan snorted. "Of course not. Obviously Phillip here has never seen someone truly lost in passion. You look like you are enjoying your meal, but when you're making love, it's better."

"Also inappropriate, Dan!" Ryan sounded strangled.

Bleu started chuckling, tickled pink. "Right. No one needs to talk about how anyone looks during sex or eating because I'm at a disadvantage."

They all hooted then, and Ryan squeezed his hand before feeding him a bit of bacon. Wow, he was having breakfast with the ex he was getting back with, the ex's ex, and his other ex....

Wait, was Phil the ex's ex if Ryan wasn't an ex anymore?

If Ryan wasn't an ex, did that make him a why?

Christ, he had a headache.

"Hey, here's your coffee." Ryan wrapped his hands around a mug.

"Mmm. Thank you. I do love Geoff's coffee. It reminds me of Santa Fe."

"You know that's where Ford's second office is, right?" Ryan told him.

"I do. I've met him in town often to check out the sculpture. I just never put Santa Fe and coffee here together."

"I haven't been to Santa Fe in years." Ryan stroked his hand.

"It hasn't changed much," Dan murmured. "The stores on the plaza change...."

"It's Santa Fe. I want to go back home to Boulder and see." Boulder had been where he'd become a man, where he'd made his first steps outside of his folks' house, where he'd learned his hardest lessons.

"I would love that. Can you take the time and come back with me?" Ryan sounded so... hopeful.

"Phil?" Dan's voice was soft.

"Hmm?"

"This is our cue to go find something amazing to do in the main house."

"But...."

"Now, buddy."

"Oh." Phil laughed. "Right." Chairs scraped, and then the door opened and shut.

"Was that bad, love?" He didn't think so, but he needed to make sure.

"No. I think Dan is just more, uh, sensitive than Phil. We're having a life discussion here."

"Yeah. Yeah, okay. Good. We're both on the same basic page, then." He ate a piece of bacon, the salt just so good. "I love you. You know that, right?"

"I think I do. I love you too. I know it sounds crazy, but I think now is our time."

"I would come with you, to learn your place. I haven't found one of my own yet. I—I want you to know that I won't be a burden to you. I do okay on my own. I'm not looking for a caretaker or a driver." He needed Ryan to know that. This wasn't about being scared for him. This was about being brave.

"Babe, I would put you and Floyd up against anyone. I'm so proud of how you've taken the reins and run with them. I'm not worried, and I want you to know I'm not scared of hooking up with the blind guy." Ryan kissed the corner of his mouth. "Mmm. Butter."

"Really?" He chased Ryan's kiss. It had almost killed him to walk away from Ryan the first time.

"Mmm-hmm. Definitely butter." Ryan kissed him again, this time full-on. He opened up, his fingers tangling in Ryan's sweater as he held on. "Come home with me. Then I'll come home with you. Then we'll decide where home is, together."

"I like the sound of that." Neither of them had a permanent home right now. Maybe they really could find where they could go together.

"So do I." Ryan hugged him with one arm. "These are really good waffles."

He found a bite with his fingers and fed Ryan the bit of sweet. Someone had been watching Ryan's every bite, but food should be sensual and happy, not guilty.

Ryan moaned softly, taking the bite and then licking his fingers clean. "God, babe. Another?"

"As much as you want."

"More, then. It tastes better from your fingers."

"Are we basking?" He thought they were basking.

"I think so. We should. You had a near-frozen experience yesterday."

"I did." But he'd been okay. He'd done well, right? They'd lived.

"So we get to be all mushy." Ryan fed him more bacon. "Besides, we have to recover some before we have sex, so why not bask?"

"Can we stay a few days? Here, I mean? Together? I want to make sure Stoney is okay, and I want to be there when he sees the statue."

"I asked Ford this morning. Everyone is clearing out today, and we can move to a cabin of our own. Dan wants to stay until tomorrow, but Phil is leaving this afternoon."

"Good. Maybe one with a hot tub?" He wanted champagne and hot tub time with Ryan. He wanted to know that his hot tub time with Ryan would end with orgasms.

"Yeah, they're giving us the honeymoon cabin." He heard the laughter lurking in Ryan's voice, and he had to chuckle too.

"Tell me there's a heart-shaped bed." His momma had told him about that, about how motels had honeymoon suites with heart-shaped magic-finger beds.

"I think it's a lodge pine king. We'll find a heart-shaped bed when we go to Vegas. I do a show there every year."

"Oh, I've never been there." He'd love to go.

"There are amazing restaurants and all sorts of crazy shows you could hear as well as experience."

He loved that Ryan just accepted that he could come along, that he would be welcome. "Thank you."

"You know it. I have a few things in February, but we'll figure out schedules, huh? I don't want you to get behind on work."

Bleu loved the sound of that. February and beyond. "We'll find a studio, or a place where I can have one." That was always best.

"Yeah. Someplace with lots of space, right? You do some big pieces."

"I do." He fed Ryan another bite, tracing his lover's lips.

"Then we find something with the right kind of studio." Ryan said it firmly, and he grinned.

This was definitely lovers basking, but Ryan was absolutely right. They totally deserved it.

After all, he'd damn near froze his nuts off just yesterday.

Chapter Twenty-Two

THEY had a wee unveiling party Monday afternoon for Stoney and Bleu.

Geoff made pizza, Ford mixed crazy hot Bloody Marys, and Bleu got to be there the first time Stoney saw the statue.

Ryan was about to bust a gut, he was so proud. Bleu couldn't see Stoney's face, but his expression was one of pure awe.

The statue was Ford's and Stoney's hands, their wedding rings clear, clasped over the nose of Stoney's mare, the main house underneath the horse's chin. Stoney's lips tightened as he reached out, touching their clasped hands. "Well… I'll be goddamned, honey. Look at this."

Bleu grinned, and Ryan could see that no one needed to tell Bleu he'd done good. Bleu heard.

"It's great, yeah?" Ford held Stoney's hand. "It's us. The ranch. Everything."

"It's beautiful. Seriously. It's.... Thank you." Stoney looked up to Ford, who cupped the angular bruised face and took a long, deep kiss.

Ryan almost felt like an intruder, at least until Doogie and Quartz burst out with an "Ewwwww!"

Bleu nudged him. "What did I miss?"

"Stoney and Ford playing movie heroes and kissing. Very dramatic." He forgot Bleu needed the play-by-play.

"Aww. Yay! That's the best ending."

"Sap," Tanner muttered.

"Duh," Bleu shot back.

"Also gay, so it's nice to see gay smoochies," Ryan added.

Tanner made exaggerated gagging noises, then oofed when Geoff whacked his butt.

"Geoff is spanking Tanner," Ryan said sotto voce.

"I thought Tanner was the straight one?"

"I am!"

They all began to laugh, just cackling like hyenas as they stood there in the main lobby.

"Who wants pizza?" Geoff asked.

"Has anyone in the history of the earth ever said no to your pizza?" Bleu grinned in Geoff's direction.

"Thank you." Geoff came over to smack a kiss on Bleu's unbruised cheek.

Ryan grinned and wrapped one arm around Bleu's waist, leading his lover back toward the kitchen. "You did good, babe."

"Thank you." Bleu grinned wide. "He likes it."

"He loves it. Very much. Lunch and then our cabin?"

That grin just got bigger. "Hot tub?"

"God yes. Maybe we could take lunch to go." That wouldn't offend anyone, would it?

"Let me whisper in Geoff's ear."

Ryan handed Bleu over, and before he knew it, Geoff had a box with a pizza, a bottle of chianti, and two pieces of cheesecake. Fuck yes.

He half carried Bleu, while Bleu carried lunch. Floyd stayed with Quartz, who looked tickled pink to be trusted with the mutt again.

"Have fun, boys!" Stoney called, and Bleu answered with a happy laugh.

He waved with his free hand, just chuckling madly. Everyone knew they were heading off to make love.

Especially his Bleu.

They wandered over to their cabin, which was a little out of the way, a little isolated in the snow. The views were stunning, but with Bleu it was all about the quiet. He said it was incredibly peaceful.

More than that, they could be loud together and no one would care.

One of his favorite things about Bleu was the happy sounds that heralded his pleasure.

They made it inside, where Ryan set the food on the dining table before swinging Bleu gently into his arms. "Hot tub."

"Hot tub. Bubbles. Nakedness."

Wherever they landed, he was totally getting them a hot tub. His lover was an addict.

They undressed, and he winced at the bruises Bleu still wore. They weren't hurting so bad, Bleu said, but they were in the lurid phase.

It seemed like every day he found another one too. Thank goodness Dan was gone or Bleu'd be wrapped in Bubble Wrap.

He grinned at the idea of a plastic-wrapped Bleu bobbing in the hot tub.

Ryan got everything bubbling away while Bleu brought over towels and robes and draped them over the warmer, then grabbed a couple of bottles of water.

"Anything else?"

"I'll make sure lube and all is out by the bed." He wasn't teasing. This was necessary.

"Perfect." Bleu nodded and slipped into the water, head back on the padded side.

He threw off the rest of his clothes so he could climb in as well, the lovely heat almost shocking after being outside. It took about two seconds for Bleu to float over to him, to straddle his lap and press close.

"Hey." He grabbed that tight ass, not squeezing too hard, but jonesing on the closeness.

"Hello, love." Bleu reached back and pulled his hair out of his ponytail, the mass surrounding them like a curtain.

"Mmm. This is so much better than the big hot tub."

"Mmm-hmm. This is…." A huge bubble popped up between them, and Bleu threw his head back with a happy laugh.

"I know, right?" Ryan was laughing along, his whole body swaying with it.

"Oh, that felt amazing. Did it tickle you too?"

"It so did." That was silly and wonderful.

"We're going to Boulder tomorrow. I can't wait. You'll have to take me to get burgers."

"God yes. I want to watch you eat one. I know we had burgers here, but the Sink! I can't wait." He began to massage Bleu's ass, fingertips digging in, drawing them together. Bleu's face went lax, tongue flicking out to wet those parted lips.

Hoo yeah. Someone was really feeling better.

"You like that, babe?"

"More, Ryan. I want to feel more."

Feeling better and greedy for him, all at once.

"I want all the things, but we can take them one at a time." He traced the crease down, pressing a tiny bit.

"You can take everything you want. One or two at a time." Bleu leaned in, biting his earlobe hard enough that his eyes crossed.

"We're supposed to be bubbling and relaxing," Ryan teased.

"Uh-huh. You're not relaxed?" Bleu spread even wider for him.

"Parts of me are very tense." He rubbed up, letting Bleu feel his hardness.

"Mmm." Bleu moaned and grabbed him, bold as brass, measuring him from base to tip. "I have never forgotten this, love. Not once."

"No. I never forgot any of it." Ryan kissed Bleu's mouth, wanting his love to feel it. He wrapped one hand around the back of Bleu's head, tilting him so their tongues could tangle.

Bleu wrapped both arms around his neck, holding on tight, and he missed the grip on his cock. There was nothing like those clever fingers with their heavy calluses to make him lose his mind.

He moaned when Bleu nibbled his lower lip, then his chin.

"Hungry lover," Ryan said.

"Yes. I could eat you up." Bleu moved slow as molasses, teeth stinging his throat.

"Okay, yes." They could totally do that. Once they got out of the water. He pushed the hair from Bleu's face, needing to see everything.

Bleu reached up to touch his cheeks, looking at him too. "Only fair."

"I agree, babe." Ryan smiled, feeling so easy in his skin, so damn happy.

Bleu's moan filled the air, and the joy in his lover's face made his balls draw up tight. Christ, Bleu loved him. Still. No bullshit, no lies, no hesitation. Just hunger and need and forever.

He jerked, his hips rising and falling. "We should go to bed before I make a mess, babe."

"Yes. We can soak again after. I want you. I want everything."

He nodded, then pushed up to help Bleu out of the tub. That ankle was still a little unstable. Bleu followed his lead, at least until they got to the bed; then Ryan was spread out, Bleu's hands on him, searching him, mapping out every single hot spot he knew he had, plus a dozen no one else had been patient enough to find.

Ryan panted, moving his hips, his chest heaving. "You going to do me this time, babe?"

"You know it. I'm going to make you so happy." Bleu licked at his belly, slick fingers pressing into him without a hint of warning. When had Bleu even found the lube? Crazy good.

He spread, digging into the mattress with his heels. Ryan hadn't been joking about making a mess, so he was glad Bleu wasn't wasting time.

"Mine." Bleu's fingers liked to turn him inside out. God, they knew exactly where to touch.

"Yours." There was no arguing about that. As quick as it had been, he was Bleu's, body and soul. Maybe he always was and he just hadn't been smart enough or adult enough.

Whatever it was, Bleu was inside him, to the bone.

All he could do was bear down and let Bleu open him up, get him ready. He wanted everything.

When Bleu pulled away, he groaned, suddenly empty and aching.

"I'm coming back. Let me slick up."

"Hurry, babe. Imma die." Dramatic? Sure. He needed Bleu.

Bleu chuckled. "Oh, now. It would be a shame to pass over preorgasm."

"Right?" He ran his hands over his belly and chest, his nipples so hard they were too sensitive for the slightest caress.

"I can smell how you need me." Bleu kneeled up tall, that proud erection in one hand, shining with lube.

"Well, come and get me, babe." He reached out, running his finger over the head, feeling how wet Bleu was. Bleu bucked for him, arching up into his touch in a gorgeous bow. "Fuck."

"Yes." Bleu leaned down, took himself in hand, and began to rub his prick over his hole, sensitizing them both.

His skin beaded up with goose bumps, his cock bobbing. Ryan hadn't let anyone do this in so long.

"Ready?" Bleu whispered before pushing in without waiting for his response, the thick head scraping in and making him moan.

"Ready," Ryan said, laughing breathlessly. "Oh, babe. More."

"Everything."

He watched Bleu's face in utter fascination as his lover began to take him. Nothing was hidden from him—not a second of need, of passion, of the pure love that Bleu felt for him.

All he could do was stare, his hands falling to grip Bleu's hips. He was probably leaving more bruises, but he couldn't help himself.

"Yes." Bleu drove into him with strong, steady strokes that threatened to stoke a fire inside him.

God, it had never been like this, not with anyone but this man.

Panting, he started rocking up to meet each thrust, the bed shaking with their movements. They were cooking with oil, and his balls were warning him it had to end soon. Too damn soon.

"Ryan." His name sounded like a prayer, like a hymn, like Bleu's fondest wish come true.

"Love you." He had to say it because it was true and it was the most important thing. There had always been love, but now he was going to fight for it.

"Yes. Fuck yes. Love." Bleu grabbed his prick and began to stroke, good and hard, not giving him any quarter. "Need you."

"I'm gonna—" That touch overloaded his already burning senses, and Ryan shot so hard his teeth rattled, his cry echoing off the ceiling beams.

"Oh. Oh, fuck." Bleu began to take him, hips thrusting wildly, sightless eyes rolling like mad.

He watched that face, memorizing every expression. Not that he was letting Bleu go anywhere without him.

There was a second where he swore Bleu was looking at him, staring right into his soul as he climaxed, offering him the universe.

His cock jerked again, trying to let him be right there with Bleu. God help him, he was utterly lost.

Bleu slumped down against him, lips on his throat. “Damn, love. That was… so good. So fucking good.”

“Good doesn’t even begin to cover it, babe. I’m scoured and dismembered.”

Bleu began to chuckle, cock jerking inside him. “I really prefer all your limbs attached.”

“Yeah? Well, you put me back together too, so we’re good.” He pulled Bleu into the curve of his body, stroking that long back.

“Do you have any tattoos?”

“What?”

“Ink. Do you have any?”

He hooted. “I have two. A snowflake on my left shoulder and a raven on my right hip.”

“Show me.”

“You’re a demanding bastard.” He drew Bleu’s hand down to his hip, helping him trace the lines of his ink. His skin goose pimpled up again as Bleu explored.

“So it’s flying?”

“Over a little mountain peak.” He pulled Bleu’s hand up to his shoulder. “This one is bigger.” He traced the snowflake with Bleu’s fingers, remembering the time he’d cut paper snowflakes so Bleu could feel what they looked like.

“I want one. Just to know what it’s like.”

“Mmm. You know, I happen to be a designer….”

Bleu’s grin was wicked, warm. “No… really? I’d wear your art in a heartbeat. I could feel it then, driven into my skin.”

His cock gave another desperate jerk. “Damn, babe.”

“I want that, okay?”

“More than,” Ryan said. He stroked Bleu’s skin, from neck to thighs as far as he could reach. “I know the perfect artist in Seattle.”

“Mmm. Excellent. We’ll go, then. After we go back to Boulder. Together.” Bleu melted against him. “Love you.”

“I love you, Bleu.” The rest was just planning and details. Good thing they both had exes who were managers and wanted to run their lives. That way he and Bleu could just be.

They had an entire world to see.

Epilogue

"THE mail, boss." Mira handed him a stack of stuff, and Ford blinked. She handled the bills, so this was all personal stuff.

"Thanks, lady." Ford sorted through it on the way to the family side of the house. Donation request. A package from Mason, which was probably samples of some sort. Two science magazines for Quartz. Huh. There was one fancy envelope, the kind he associated with graduations and wedding announcements. The return address was Boulder.

He dropped the magazines off, Quartz oblivious to his presence, headphones on, focus on his computer screen.

Ford pondered going to his office, but he heard soft singing coming from the bedroom, happy low laughter filling the air.

Oh, there was no way on earth he could resist that.

Stoney was in his skivvies, still damp from the shower. The scars from his accident were fading finally, the only noticeable change the beard he'd started wearing to hide the marks along his jaw.

"Are we dancing?" He threw the mail on the bed, grabbing Stoney's hand.

"Mmm. I know you." Stoney moved right into his arms, face lifted for a kiss. "Afternoon."

"Lazy man." He knew better. Stoney had been out working in the early spring slush. Good thing their only guest right now was a Texas singer who just wanted to sleep and soak in the hot tub. He swung Stoney into a two-step as the music changed to something King George.

"That's me." Stoney moved like a dream against him. "What you been up to?"

"Phone calls from the office. Nothing fun."

"Oh, that's no good."

"Nope, but this is. Good, I mean." He chuckled, the joy welling up in his chest just like it did every time he and Stoney got a moment to groove together.

"You know it." Stoney took another kiss, this one more promise and heat than gentle, and his body began to take notice of the fact that his husband was one pair of tighty-whities from bare-butt naked.

Ford grabbed that sweet ass, ready for more than dancing.

He grinned at Stoney when the song ended. "I think I better lock the door."

"I think that's a wonderful idea. Get rid of all the clothes while you're at it." Stoney shucked his briefs and grabbed the mail off the bed, put the pile on the bedside table.

Ford locked the door as Stoney sat on the bed and grabbed the top envelope from the pile. He stared over, and Stoney grinned.

"What? I'm waiting on your happy ass to get nekkid." Stoney opened the envelope and hooted as Ford struggled out of his sweater and turtleneck. "Looks like Bleu and Shields bought themselves a house."

"Yeah?" *Fuck. Boots before jeans, man. Boots before jeans.* "Where'd they end up?" Ford asked from the floor, where he'd tipped over.

"Boulder. Looks like they're sharing a studio there. They've invited us to a party." Stoney looked down the side of the bed at him. "You okay down there?"

"Oh, I just thought I'd check out the dust bunny situation." He pulled off one boot, then the other. "You wanna go? We could get a hotel and stay, maybe go out to eat."

"I'm all over that. We could have a long weekend, maybe go to Denver for an afternoon." Stoney put the card on top of the rest of the mail, smile going a little wicked. "We could do things that frighten fish."

"We so could." Ford wiggled out of his jeans before he stood. Probably not sexy, but convenient. "You think they'll do their wedding here?"

"I'll beat their asses if they don't. After all, we're why they hooked back up." Stoney grabbed him, using his johnson like a handle. "As much as I adore the boys, I think that the relationship I'm concerned with is much more personal right now, Mr. Nixel."

"Oof. Careful with that, Mr. River. You might need it in a minute or two." He crawled on the bed, pressing down against Stoney.

"Shit, I need it. All the time. In fact—" The smile was blinding. "—now is good for me."

"I'm on it." Any time was good for Ford, but in the off-season with the door locked and nothing pressing to do?

He could get downright inspired.

Coming in April 2019

Dreamspun Desires #79

Yes, Chef by T. Neilson

A savory slice of first love.

Simon's dad died when he was young, leaving Simon to take the reins of the family restaurant business—and the responsibility for his mother and brothers. His commitment to his duty left Simon time for little else, least of all romance.

Argentinian celebrity chef Luke Ferreya has wanted Simon since their culinary-school days, but for Simon, family always came first. Now Luke's back in Simon's life—briefly before he returns to South America—and he's determined to give Simon a sample of everything he's missed out on.

Simon's brothers are grown, and his mother is doing fine on her own, and Luke is offering a second chance for a future full of the pleasures of fine food, wine, and especially love. Without his obligations to hide behind, can Simon finally allow himself to say "Yes, Chef"?

Dreamspun Desires #80

Under His Protection by LaQuette

They can escape their enemies, but not the desire between them.

Prosecutor Camden Warren is on the fast track to professional Nirvana. With his charm, his sharp legal mind, and his father as Chief Judge in the highest court in NY, he can't fail. Nothing can derail his rise to the top...until an attempt on his life forces him to accept the help of a man he walked out on five years ago.

Wounded in the line of duty, Lt. Elijah Stephenson wants to ride his new desk job until retirement—not take a glorified babysitting gig with more risk than it's worth… especially not protecting the entitled lawyer who disappeared after the best sex of their lives.

The threat against Camden's life is real, but their passion for each other might prove the greatest danger they've yet to face.